STORIES YOU DO

NOT KNOW

by Emma Donaldson

ISBN - 13:978-1500274245

ISBN – 10:1500274240

Cover photo by Emma Donaldson

To my dear friend, Claudia,

who continues to inspire me.

Thank-you for
everything you share!
love,
E. Donaldson

Table of Contents

Androgyny

After the diagnosis, I remembered my grandfather, Poppa, crying at the kitchen table. I knew that cancer could take one's life, but his manifested in his prostate and I did not understand how it could take his manliness. It was not even his penis or testicles. To me, I understood the function of the prostate was secondary to these other organs. Perhaps the sorrow he expressed was the only way he could deal with the fears he must have had. He complained that he would not be a man anymore. I tried to understand what he was feeling, but I could not. He was old and had grandchildren. His skin hung loose on his face and hands, discolored by liver spots. Was it important to always feel like a man, even in old age? Or even a woman? In my mind, for the longest time, there seemed to be an androgynous quality that increased with age. At least that is how I saw those who aged around me.

When my brother and I were in our teens, I could almost feel the hormones emitting from him. Testosterone laden molecules that hitch-hiked on beads of sweat and filled the air with his own musky manliness. When rough-housing with other boys, like puppies and kittens acting tough with bared teeth as they barrel-rolled or somersaulted over each other, he would emanate hormones or pheromones, or stink as I identified it. Even at the kitchen table, gobbling down turkey sandwiches, or at church, held tight in bondage of his Sunday clothes that he was always growing out of, there was a distinct scent.

Then there were the men Momma would sometimes date. I did not like the way they looked at me, or Momma for that fact, with that hungry-eyed look that made me shiver between my legs. There was an uncomfortable air of dominance in their own animal musk that could not be masked by any amount of spiciness or sweetness of aftershave, but created a sour smell when mixed together.

My own husband had the same look in his eyes and scents on his skin when we courted. Dated. Fucked in the backseat of his car. Call it what you want, but that was the grim reality of my own body inebriating my brain with hormones to initiate the animal instinct to reproduce. There was even a period of time when I thought he and I invented it. But I figured I'd mature out of romance, my husband would grow out of lust and we would be like Poppa and Grandmother.

Poppa and Grandmother did not touch affectionately or kiss or stuff like that. I knew they loved each other with their minds and did not need to with their bodies anymore. But then, I never did love my husband fully with my mind. I always had to remind myself why I loved him. Escaping Momma, the baby, the house, the paycheck, the food on the table. Eventually sex was not a justification to continue loving

2

him, so apparently I was taking my first steps towards androgyny.

Poppa did not have that musky smell that conjured up lewd feelings. The pipe smoke was all the sweetness I ever wanted to smell on him and the sharp smell of diesel fuel on his hands which made him man enough in my head. And it was Poppa's love that I knew before I knew anything else which was all about me and had nothing to do with sex.

I think about these things as I wait to hear from the doctor that cancer has claimed my reproductive organs. The doctor did not say the word, but had said "...we'll do some tests to rule out the possibility of other things." Other things, I ponder. Strawberry shortcake. Dead car battery. Pebble in my shoe. I'm not sure why the doctor did not say cancer. Perhaps it would be like yelling fire in a movie theater. At least rule out everything before the word forms at the lips and changes a person's life forever. I know everything had been ruled out for Poppa when he heard the word cancer.

I catch myself holding my breath as I go through the day. If it is cancer, is it easier to remove it or do they now leave it in and do chemotherapy? I don't know. I have had no need to know until this point. Removing these organs of reproduction that have not seen a good chance of doing any reproduction in the last twenty-five years, will slide me, no doubt, into the menopausal stage I don't want to welcome so soon. Knowing the irony and absurdity, I let my mind say it out-loud and echo off the insides of my head, that excising this anatomy will take my ability to bear children. It's so silly. I now have grandchildren, for

Pete's sake. But yet, I'm not ready to succumb to the androgynous body I had thought I would eventually grow into. I still want to be a woman. My outsides and my insides intact.

Rituals

There is something about spring in the damp early days where the cold can settle back onto the land. Mother Nature might choose to set her hand down hard on the tender buds that the sunshine and warm weather has coaxed out of their protective hiding spots.

Anna lifted her face toward the light in the sky overhead and followed it like the big cheerful faces of the sunflowers that would grow tall through the summer at the north edge of Grandmother's garden. She could feel the green branches of her arms and legs flex in the wind. She could feel the pink blossoms blooming on her cheeks.

Best of all in the springtime, was climbing onto her grandfather's lap and riding out into the fields on the old red Farmall tractor. Sitting so close to him, she came to recognize his scent as the clean smell of newly turned field dirt mixed with the sweet clean smell of fresh split wood. She could still smell him through the exhaust coming from the sieved smokestack that was blackened by soot and heated gunmetal blue. Poppa's arms would stretch around her as he gripped the steering wheel. She felt the warm ropy muscles of his forearms against her own that looked pale and fragile against his. She imagined his arms flexing and sweat beading up on his skin and matting the hair down in the late summer as he would swing bales of hay or straw onto a flatbed truck. If his arms had made sounds, they would have sounded like the low chug of the tractor motor. Instead, they were always gentle when she sat in their protective embrace.

In the springtime, Poppa would hook up the plow and create furrows in the fields of winter wheat. Over and over, the tractor would go back and forth over the field, creating a moist, loamy corduroy that would softly drape the landscape from the top of the hill down to where the field turned to muck at the edge of the swail.

The green in the swail was dying back more and more each year. The Sand Hill Cranes had stopped visiting the spot to rest in the brushy cover. The spring peepers lost their volume until it had become silence. She watched her grandfather stare at the natural chaos, as if he stared hard enough, he could will the marshy plants thriving and the animal sounds to return to its usual music.

She accepted the change in the swampy area of the field that could not be used for crops because she had yet to understand that she could change as much too. She was at the age where life radiated outward from where she stood in the present. It was her childhood belief that things and events that had happened to her would continue to happen forever and into the future. For instance, she knew later that summer, the Farmall would haul the sprayer through the potato field across the road, and she and her brother would sneak up behind the tractor to feel the mist fall on their tanned skin in the bright sunshine, evaporating and creating momentary coolness.

A heady sweet smell rose from the turned over dirt. She knew this sweet, sweet smell translated into the milky sap of the corn that would be grown. In the summer, she would sneak out to the corn fields with her brother and nibble on an ear of corn. He instructed her how to carefully pick an ear without breaking the stalk and then burying the nibbled cob below the surface of the dirt. Poppa planted it, but Grandmother would be mad, telling the children they were wasting hard earned money. The corn needed to grow all summer and turn hard and dry on the stalks. It would be harvested and sold to the grain elevator in the fall.

Knee-high by the Fourth of July. She had been taught the saying as a measure of the corn stalks growth. It was not until the tassels reached far overhead that it was fun to walk through the corn rows and believe it was a jungle forest dense along the Amazon. The long dry leaves would cut at the skin on arms and legs while the pollen would fall off the tassels, dusting cheeks and noses to sneezes. The dirt between the rows would rise in dusty swirls, kicked up by rubber soled sneakers. The shade between the stalks was dense enough at the lower level, but oppressive as it stifled any cooling breezes at the edge of the field. The tops of the tassels danced in defiance, reveled and moved with the wind, showing off what they had been allowed to rise to, over the rest.

It was another world inside the perimeter of the cornfield that grew and defined the yard where the house and barn sat. The soft caressing of the leaves, over and over and over, hypnotized her into thinking

7

she was safe, hidden among a sea of greenness, and she was as strong and rooted as the corn sentinels lined up in parade rows.

Standing in the tall corn she would remember every spring when Poppa would pull her close while driving the tractor with the plow dragging behind, and feel the first moist drops wet her auburn hair. They would join others and eventually trickle down her face like her own tears. She knew they were not like the drops from a spring rain that left everything new and fresh, but they would have caused pain in her own wounds with the saltiness they contained. She never dared look up or turn around and face her grandfather or pull away from his embrace. She knew this had become their ritual, their tradition, something they shared together, intimately, the tears she knew her grandfather only shed each spring.

School Days

Big Brother heard his mother calling for him to wake up. He sat up and let his whole body yawn out the rest of his sleepiness. He crossed his legs and said his morning prayers. *Thank-you Mother Earth and Father Sky for the home you give me. Thank-you Great Spirit for letting me wake again for another day. Thank-you for my mother who bore me and my father who guides me.* He was old enough to fold his own blanket, which he did after shaking it out.

After eating the food his mother gave him, he went and gathered sticks for the fire. Soon this would be Little Brother's responsibility. He had been trying to teach him to find the sticks that snapped crisp between forcing hands. Those would be dry and would give quick fire. Twigs that resisted breaking were still green and would slow a fire down. Other wood, when burned, would scent the smoke with its spirit.

In the thicket, Big Brother heard crying. It sounded like Little Brother, hiding his sorrow in stifled sobs. He looked past the trees, looking for a hint of Little Brother's light brown hair. He kept looking and looking. The sobs did not change by getting softer or louder as he moved silently over the ground.

He did not want to call out to his brother, afraid that he would hide, trying to find solace alone, ashamed to be crying. Little Brother was so competitive and wanted to be brave like Big Brother. Part of becoming a brave warrior was learning to ask the spirits to carry away any sorrow that weighed the heart down. He sat quietly and would let Little Brother find him when he was done crying and maybe they would go hunting or fishing.

He knew Little Brother liked to follow him down to the stream and sit quietly on the log that overhung the water. Big Brother would lie on the log, belly side, with his arms dangling so his hands flowed with the current of the stream. Occasionally, fish swimming by would not take notice of his hands until after he had caught one. They would take it back to their mother and she would cover it with clay and slip it into the fire and bake it. The brothers could almost taste the tender flesh that gave a light fragrance of the lake from the steam which rose from it before the clay was cracked open.

Little Brother also liked to follow Big Brother to where the heart berries grew, the *ode'iminan*, and check their ripeness. The serrated leaves would tease over the bashful berries, hiding them sometimes. They were tiny burst of sweetness released along with the bitter crunch of golden seeds freckling the red flesh. The brothers would report their findings to Mother and she and her sisters and girl cousins and the other women would go and gather the berries to dry in the sun on the reed baskets.

Being a big brother had responsibility. It was important to show Little Brother a good example of taking care of oneself, but in the mean time, Big Brother would protect him until he understood the dangers that surrounded them. He knew he had to be brave, act brave, show that he was, so Little Brother would know what it meant to be a man.

There were so many things Big Brother was teaching Little Brother, like the tracks of the woodland animals, the split hooves of the deer and the serpentine line where a snake had traveled. Most important, he was teaching Little Brother to stay quiet, unobtrusive between the trees and amongst the wind. Later Big Brother would teach him other signs of animal paths and teach him to hunt each animal for food.

Standing in the forest looking for Little Brother dissolved in his mind as a squeak from another boy's bed broke Big Brother's dream. He still heard Little Brother's stifled sobbing across the room, where they now lived in Iowa. So far away from their home under the forest canopy in Michigan with the lakes and streams. So far away from their mother and father, here in the flat lands where the eye tired from its travel from the east horizon to the west. The trees were left behind, except for some scrubby trees called cottonwoods that grew on the banks of the creeks filled with muddy water when there was any flow. The white fluff would blow across the prairie in the late spring and pretend to be drifts of snow.

Big Brother missed his parents. He missed the way his mother would rub oils into his skin making it soft and creating a barrier against the bugs, especially the *zagimeg* that liked to bite and draw blood. He missed the way father would take him aside to teach him how to pound the dusky slate until they were knapped into sharp arrow points. It did not matter if he opened his eyes or left them closed, he could still see the faces of his parents. But his mother's eyes, the last time he had looked into them, he did not understand. They were empty in the sea of tears. His grandfather, a respected warrior in the tribe, had held his body limp with defeat, with anger being the only strength and determination on his face. No one spoke of Father and why he did not come home. Big Brother did not understand their faces when they had embraced him hard and told him to be brave and take care of his brother. Their sadness could not be hidden and was a contradiction which left no room for him to remember their smiles.

The Great Father in Washington had sent a teacher, who was also a clergyman, a respected man in the pale face's esteem. Brother Michael smiled at the mothers and fathers, but not looking into their eyes when he told them he would take care of the children. Big Brother and Little Brother and many other boys and girls whom the pale faces called Indians and sometimes savages or heathens or redskins, had been loaded into metal boxes with windows you could see through but could not feel the breeze across your face or smell the scent of flowers from a meadow in bloom. The children were pulled by iron horses that the pale facess called locomotives and followed two metal tracks called rails. All the children were timid of the locomotive. It puffed hard as it got started, like a boy carrying too heavy of a load. When the train sped along the endless expanse of prairie, it chugged with a smooth rhythm like when the boys raced with each other. When the iron horse came to a stop, its steam engine hissed, releasing white clouds up in the sky for a change from the black, like a sigh of a boy whose legs collapsed at the end of a big run. The locomotive was alive but without a spirit and that bothered the children. They knew people who were alive, but whose spirit had left them. There was nothing to keep them from doing wrong.

The boys did not like Brother Michael who had accompanied them on the train. He was sweaty most of the time, pulling a white cloth from his black jacket and dabbing the moisture from his forehead. Unlike Sister Angeline, who they would later meet, Brother Michael never looked the boys in the face and smiled, but looked at them with hungry eyes. They disliked the way he touched their arms and their backs and shoulders. They did not trust his hungry eyes. That was a look one might have when watching a *waabooz,* with its long ears and twitching nose, hopping along, and thinking of tasting the flesh turned tender from the flame. To look at a person like that was suspect. Brother Michael could not roast the boys, but maybe he wanted to devour something more precious than flesh, perhaps coveting after their spirits.

At the school, they were introduced to new adults.

"I am Father Xavier. Listen to what I say," said the man that made Brother Michael nervous. "You are to follow the rules and learn how to be civilized."

Father Xavier instructed the Sisters to take away the children's filthy possessions. Possessions included everything they had brought with them and everything they were wearing. Each child was given a different shirt, pair of trousers and little pants with short legs called underwear, and shoes that pinched their toes, not allowing the bottoms of their feet to feel the earth they walked upon. After changing into the new clothes, the old ones were whisked away by the 'Sisters' who dressed alike with black and white draped over them, only their faces peaked out.

Father Xavier seemed to be the father of the Sisters and Brother Michael. They always called him 'father' when they asked him for permission to do something or took orders from him. He even required all the little Indian boys and girls to call him 'father.' Some children who understood a little English, giggled at calling him father, until his face turned deep red and he erupted into yelling. He marched over to one of the boys who had giggled and grabbed him roughly by the arm and dragged him to the front of the room. Father pushed the boy down to his knees and started whipping his backside with a black snake that snapped in the air with an earsplitting crack. The boy fell forward, his hands catching him. The boys and girls could see him biting his lip, but he dared not cry out or let the tears drip from his eyes. The girls bowed their heads and the boys braced themselves, waiting for a signal to go save a fellow warrior from this unfounded punishment. The father sensed this and took a step towards the children and waved the black snake at them. They were scared of it even though Big Brother saw that it was leather braided together and the flicking tongue was really the ends of the braid, like his own mother's hair.

Father Xavier yelled at the children. He was so angry and they could not understand his words. Only later, after hearing them hundreds of times each day from the sisters, would the children understand words like 'discipline,' 'savages,' 'civilized,' 'obedience,' and

"You are forbidden to speak anything but English."

No one spoke anything until he signaled to the Sisters and he himself left the room. The boys and girls were separated and the girls were led out of the room. Sister Angeline was left with the boys and helped the boy who had been whipped, back to the group. She looked at him, lifted his chin and made him look into her eyes.

"You must listen to Father Xavier," she told him. "You must follow the rules."

She repeated herself over and over as she went through the group of boys, lifting chins as she went. Her voice was soft and her eyes were begging. The boys listened to her. She was nice and they wanted to please her. Sister Therese-Marie with her skin hanging on her bones and her black gown hanging on her body like it had been thrown over a couple of upright sticks, glared at her, but did not do anything, perhaps recognizing the savage look on the boy's faces as loyalty, like on a dog's face. She made an unpleasant sound and informed them they would go to the next building and have their hair cut. No one knew what that was until the first boy, whose shiny black hair had been braided down his back, was no longer.

Sister Therese-Marie held a shiny silver thing in her hand and opened its beak and it bit down on the boy's hair and made a soft thump when it hit the floor. The boys gasped and the boy did not realize what had happened until he saw the braid next to his feet. He picked it up gently and looked at it and then took steps towards Sister Therese-Marie who still had the sharp beak in her hand. He yelled at her and it was not English. How dare she do that. Would she take is arm next? His leg? More Sisters came running in with Brother Michael. The silver flashed around the room as Sister Therese-Marie walked towards the boy, yelling. Brother Michael grabbed the boy around the middle and held him tight while the other Sister held his arms. The boy fought and thrashed, until blood ran down the side of his face. The sharp beaks must have cut him. They let go of him and he dejectedly hung his head and slumped his shoulders as he walked across the room and collapsed in the corner.

The sisters were ready for their next victim. One of the boys yelled scalping into the chaos as they chased him around the room. He held his hands tight to the top of his head as Brother Michael grinned deliciously at the boy and grabbed him with quick arms.

Many of the boys cried after their hair was cut. Some tried to pick up their braids, only to have one of the sisters snatch it out of their hands. They cried with pure sorrow behind their wails. They were brave boys growing to be brave men who did not cry, but with their hair cut, they lost their strength. Later on, they would know how Samson felt when Delilah cut his hair, they discovered when one of the Sisters read them the story from the Bible. She slapped the book closed when one of the boys pointed that out and they never heard the story again.

Big Brother worried that Little Brother loved the Bible stories so much that he might forget the stories their own father use to tell them. It hurt to remember how Grandfather would tell stories all winter long, his favorite being when Grandfather would wave his arm behind him, showing how the tail of the coyote swished.   But those stories Father Xavier carried around in his black book he called the Bible, he insisted were not stories, but the word of God. And God created everything. That, the boys could believe. Just like Mother Earth. Then there was Mary, mother of Jesus. Her kind eyes and soft smile from the pictures and statues made Big Brother think of Sister Angeline. Mary had to be like their Mother Earth. When Father Xavier asked the boys who was the son of God, Little Brother raised his hand correctly, like the Sisters had taught them all.

"I am, Father," Little Brother said, proud to know the answer. Father Xavier started getting red.

"No," he shouted. "You are not. Jesus Christ is his only begotten son."

The rest of the boys sat silently and looked at the floor. Little Brother's answer had made sense to them. Were they not all God's creating, which made them all his children? At least that is how their parents had taught them that they were all children of Mother Earth and Father Sky. That is how the elders of the tribe had taught them. Father Xavier could be heard mumbling about God testing whether or not he could save these heathen souls from the devil.

This devil, described in the pale faces book, terrified the children, as they had never been told such frightening stories before. Repeatedly, they were told that evil lurked in every direction, leaving the children to look cautiously behind themselves for the ugly and scary features that they were constantly reminded of. Whenever Father Xavier or the Sisters would make reference to the devil, Big Brother would picture and evil man with eyes like Brother Michael.

Farming

At the farm, Anna felt like she was at home. Grandmother and Poppa had always been farmers, but they had only owned the farm a year before Anna's older brother, Nick, had been born. So whenever Anna and Nick were dropped off at the farm, which was often, Grandmother's critical eyes and tongue, Poppa's bear hugs and the field dirt that collected under Anna's fingernails, comforted her, knowing this was hers.

Sharecroppers was a description that most would reserve for negroes, but Grandmother and Poppa were white folk and they rented. There never seemed to be any money to save for the farm from the pittance they received. Anna's mom and Uncle Weston got jobs at the factory when they each turned eighteen. Within a few years, there was enough money for a down payment on the forty acres. When Uncle Wes told the story, he always poked at Anna's mother, "would 'ave been sooner if your momma hadn't bought so many purty dresses." To which she would retort, "I was done wearing rags."

Anna never heard her grandparents say they were proud of their modest farm, but they were careful of always putting tools back, making tidy rows in the garden and keeping the buildings painted and the fences mended. Anna would not realize this was what pride felt like until she grew up and owned something of her own. As a child, Anna found their attitude to feel like hard work.

Momma explained when Grandmother and Poppa bought the farm, the house was a wreck and the yard a jungle. The old garden had been a dump with broken dishes, whisky bottles, old bones and even a fender off a car. Grandmother refused to have her yard look like a junk yard. So many a day, Poppa and Uncle Wes dismantled the haven for snakes and turned it into a garden patch. Momma recalled how she scrapped paint off the sides of the clapboarded sides of the house, standing on a ladder with Nick poking her belly out.

They planted fruit trees in rows and by the time Anna was old enough to play in the yard, the crowns of the trees had grown together. In the spring she would walk down between the trees and pretend she was a bride with a dress as delicate as the petals and a blush to her cheeks and lips the color of the peach blossoms. The buzz of bees, Anna imagined, was the hum of people filling the pews and whispering about how beautiful she looked. The ends of the limbs reaching to the next tree was the roof of the church, soaring up like a cathedral. Rarely would she consider a man at the altar, but when she did, glimpses of Poppa ran through her mind.

In the front yard, a big oak tree stood grandly, shading the house from the hot summer sun. Quite often, Anna and her brother would explore the furthest reaches of the farm. Today she played under the tree by herself. Nick had gone swimming with a friend who

19

lived on the lake. Pleasantly enough Anna asked her mother to let her go too. Her brother gloated and made faces behind their mother's back while she got ready for work that morning. Anna resorted to crying and yelling "it's not fair," as she stamped her feet, blowing hot anger out of her nostrils like a mad bull.

A swat on her behind made the tears real and Anna sat moping under the tree with her pride still stinging from her mother's strong hand. There was a patch of thin bladed grass in the shape of an oval rug and when Nick and the cousins were there, they pushed each other off, vying for a spot. The blades felt velvety and cool under her fingertips. She sprawled out on her belly, relishing the coolness next to her sweaty and sticky skin. She found an acorn cap from last season and toyed with it on the tips of her fingers.

Anna paid little attention to the truck coming down the road with a cloud of dust following it. The green pickup slowed down and pulled into the driveway.

"Your grandfather here?" the man asked as he got out of his truck. It was Hal Hudson from down the way.

"He's out back," Anna said. Poppa was coming out of the barn and greeted Hal. They leaned against the truck and the low timbre of their conversation bored Anna. Farmer talk about crops, animals and weather. It could go on and on to the point of ignoring small voices that said "Poppa, I have to pee."

Anna remembered when she was little and she and Nick and Cousin Donny had gone with Poppa to look at another farmer's crop that was not faring well.

"Dunno why this field is so weak," he told

Poppa.

"You gotta grow something else other than corn on this dirt for a while."

"Something else? I farm corn. Not something else."

"Poppa," Anna interrupted. "I gotta pee."

"Hate to see your crop fail, but that's what I suggest."

"Good corn was grown on this field before I got it. How come it fails me?" he shook his head back and forth.

Anna went back to Nick and Donny. They were far from any house, much less an outhouse, which many farm houses in the area still had as their main bathroom. Anna sighed that there was not even a lousy tree to squat behind in the middle of the cornfield with yellowed shoots no higher than her ankles. Her bladder succumbed to the pain and took over. She was not in control anymore. Warm ran down her leg and into her sneaker. A wet spot grew in the crotch of her shorts. Nick and Donny stared at her. Then Anna noticed Donny's pants getting wet between his legs. What could Nick do, refusing to be left out?

"Looks like your kids pissed themselves," the farmer said to Poppa.

"Better get you kids home," he said sheepishly and started for the truck. Poppa still playfully tossed Anna into the truck bed, even though her pants were wet. She sat down on the wheel hump with Nick and Donny sitting across from her on the other hump.

"Anna," Poppa's voice broke into her thoughts and brought her back to under the oak tree. "Tell your grandmother you're going to Hal's with me."

"How come?" she asked.

"He's got a sick cow."

Anna ran to the back door and yelled the message through the screen door, barely waiting for Grandmother to reply. She was excited to go with Poppa. It made her feel grown-up and responsible. Grandmother always said the kids needed to keep their lips buttoned when adults were doing business. Anna kept quiet while Poppa looked at Hal's sick cow. After much discussion, Poppa turned to Anna.

"You go wait for me in the truck." Anna obeyed and watched Hal go into his house and then come back out and go behind the barn where she could not see him or Poppa or the sick cow.

The sound of a gunshot startled Anna. The crack of sound was all too familiar from deer season in the fall. But this was not fall. It was just the beginning of August, one whole month before school started. She wondered what happened and then her thoughts rambled until she came to her brother's favorite joke to tell. "What's the difference between a bull and a steer?" he would say. "Bull's a lucky cow." Anna did not get it.

The door of the blue Ford truck creaked as Poppa got into it. Turning onto the road, Anna dared to speak.

"Did he shoot the cow?"

"Uh-huh."

"Was it that sick?"

"Uh-huh."

"How come he didn't call the vet like when Bixby's horse was sick?"

"Cause it cost too much money."

"I don't get it," Anna admitted as she bumped

up and down on the seat from the washboard on the dirt road.

"A sick cow just don't give milk. A sick horse on the other hand can't work and is therefore more valuable."

Poppa knew so much about animals. If anyone had a sick animal, they would ask Poppa first what he thought before they enlisted the services of a vet. During calving, Poppa would be gone a lot, helping who ever had fetched him. He would come home tired and empty handed, but periodically, those he helped would drop off produce, venison, or beef.

Anna knew that questioning about what went on would just earn her Grandmother's usual explanation, "This is a farm, what might not seem right for one is right for the rest." If Grandmother was particularly short on patience she would announce to everyone and no one at the same time "life isn't fair." But, per usual, this was another one of her grandmother's lessons Anna would have to learn on her own.

Savage Slaughter

Home was a ceiling of changing blue, white, grey and black with the floor a lush carpet of soft green. Family was of the old, the warriors, the women and all the children like her for the girl known as Wild Wind. Mother was the earth and Father was the sky and the Great Spirit surrounded them. Every person in the tribe had a responsibility like every rock and every leaf on each tree had a purpose. The world seemed to be a path from the home they made in the summer, back to the home they made in the winter, but always following the buffalo. But even that was changing, as the Great Father of the white man had corralled the Hunkpapa, Ogalala, and Minneconju Sioux onto tiny bits of land called reservations.

It was a cloudless morning, extraordinary, like each morning where the Great Sprit had allowed the sun to rise again, letting the moon and stars rest for the day. By the time the evening song of birds and wind would come, her world and her family, as she knew it, would be destroyed. So much fire, so much crying and blood would surround her and she would be scooped up by a pale face who looked different, sounded different, smelled different and took her away from her home.

What would be left became the slumped forms of people she had called her family, and only the teepee poles standing as smoldering skeletons of what once was their home.

It was the Indian, Wonkova, who told the great prophecy to his people who were tired, cold, starved and hunted. It seemed to make no difference for any of the Indian Nations if they fought viciously or gently tried to share, negotiated or compromised with the white man. Conversely, the Manifest Destiny prophecy of the white man justified the death of Indians and extinction of their culture also. But the Indians did not want to die and the spirit dancers sang of hope for their people. They danced in hope for the return of dead loved ones, hope for return of the white man to their own lands, hope for return of the buffalo who gave them life, provided them with food and warmth from their hides. They beaded and embroidered eagles and buffalos to the brightly colored ghost shirts that would protect them from white man bullets and genocide, a word that would not be invented until the next century to describe man's atrocities against another, and ethnic cleansing, another word that would not be invented for several more decades, as if man needed a new name to describe old hatred.

As Wild Wind watched her mother and father prepare for the spirit dance, the Ghost Dance as the whites had dubbed it, she could feel the excitement and the anticipation. She was not allowed to attend such a sacred ceremony, being just a child. She would stay with the other children, under the watchful eye of the grandmothers who would stay behind. During the day she played with the other children, but that night, she could hear, from the autumn winds, the sound of drumming from the spirit dance. Even though she did not go, she felt a part of the ceremony anyhow, letting her breath and her heartbeat follow the pattern of drumming.

She was old enough to recognize the pattern of drumming for the hunting ceremony. The drums beat out the stealth and skill needed from each of the warriors. The drumbeat would also remind them of the nourishment the animals would bring the tribe and the warm skins that would keep the tribe warm in the cold and bitter months of winter, but most importantly, there were thanks in the drumbeats, knowing without the sacrifice from the animals, their own hearts would quit beating.

Those same drums could speak of celebration also. The women would parade around the fire and dance the same dance their grandmothers had danced. The young girls would allow their bodies to tease pretty like flower petals swaying in the breeze, trying to gain the attention of the young men, especially those who offered nonchalance.

Unfortunately, she also knew the beat of the war ceremony, where the drum would beat out stories of strength and medicine which would protect the women and children and ensure that their tribe would survive and continue to exist. Instead of thanks, there was begging in the drum beats for the spirits to be with the warriors as they faced their enemies.

Whenever she was sick, the drumming and the song of the shaman were hypnotic. She was able to focus on that, until everything else fell away from her mind. The drumming when started was not supposed to stop until the end of the ceremony, whether it was for a hunt or a war or sickness. Like the heart that beat in every living thing, including the trees and the sky and everything in between, there was a beginning and an end. The drums were silent after the ceremonies, but inside each person, their hearts beat in sync, in a rhythm that had been set by the thundering sounds of the drums mimicking the sky when the lightning bolts danced.

Wild Wind was not only happy to see her parents return after the Ghost Dance, but was reassured as she saw a renewed sense of hope sparkle in their eyes, and confidence broaden their shoulders. Her mother held her tight during the night, whispering into her ear that they would no longer have to be afraid, that when the white man left and the buffalo returned, they would not be hungry anymore. She could feel her mother's excitement when she squeezed her tighter, there was hope to give her strength.

The autumn moons had passed and the first winter moon had risen when the Minneconju Tribe made their way to Cherry Cheek to draw rations and annuity goods. It was there when a few members of the Hunkpapa band from the Standing Rock Reservation sought refuge with the Minneconju. They reported soldiers had killed their chief, Sitting Bull, while they had escaped the slaughter. The Minneconju chief, Spotted Elk, also called Big Foot by the pale faces, decided to meet with Chief Red Cloud at the Pine Ridge Reservation, hoping for his people's safety amongst the chaos, as it was rumored new columns of soldiers were following the path of the sun in the east to the prairies.

For both chiefs, their words were the weapons they hoped to use to obtain peace. The journey for Spotted Elk's people had been cold and fast, little time to rest or eat, ironic since they had very little available to eat. Colonel Sumner's soldiers intercepted their journey and demanded that they would escort the band, all the people Wild Wind called family, the rest of the way to the agency. They trudged on until a wagon wheel of one of the families had caught on a fence, to which the soldiers became upset at the delay, not realizing it was accidental and not a ploy. As the soldiers waved their guns towards the disturbance, the women threw possessions and lodge poles from the wagons, worried that they needed to make the wagons lighter if they were to escape. The Minneconjus and the soldiers regained order and they continued on. After crossing Wounded Knee Creek, the tribe was directed to camp along the crest within view of the Pine Ridge Agency. Now their Chief, Spotted Elk lay confined in his teepee, dangerously ill.

This was war, and for a young girl who had seen the passage of the seasons only seven times, it was frightening to be in the middle of what should have been between men. War was supposed to be between the men of her tribe against another, or the white men. They were supposed to fight their battles away from the women and children, protect them from what the brave warriors had trained for.

There were stories exchanged between the adults when they thought the children were sleeping. It was in this way when Wild Wind would lay still with her ears dancing as she heard about how her mother's parents were driven from the east and forced to beg other tribes for acceptance, for inclusion into a family and a village again, for their own was hunted and viciously slaughtered until only a handful of the Indians from the east with blue eyes and lighter hair had nothing left to call their own.

Wild Wind could feel the apprehension crowding the clear blue skies like invisible clouds. The cold had settled close to her bones and her belly cried to be filled. She had been told she was old enough to not complain about what everyone else was already feeling. Seven cycles of the sun and moon marking their travel from their home on the Cheyenne River had left them cold, tired and hungry, and feeling hunted indiscriminately like the buffalo the white men sought for trophies, while leaving the rest of the carcass to rot on the open land.

The next morning, the white men came through the Minneconju camp looking for guns. A thickness settled over the camp and grew until Wild Wind thought she would not be able to breathe. Feelings of danger and premonition made her body feel pulled apart. Then the crack of a gunshot was heard. All around her, it seemed, as she turned and turned, the cries of her people filled her ears. Throughout the village, people were running along crazy paths only to stop suddenly with blood flowing like spilt water, everywhere until there were puddles. The drums in her heart became weaker and she could not focus on the cadence for the distracting sounds of the white men with their savage yells and the exploding sounds of their guns, the sharp cracks of the rifles and pistols they held in their hands and the low groans of the guns with wheels that had been pushed to the edge of the ridge and pointed accusatorily at them. The Cavalry came over the knoll of dying green like a bank of clouds across the blue sky, bringing with it, thunder and lightning. When the explosion with unseen waves of sound knocked her to her feet, Wild Wind could only hear an unnatural buzzing not in her ears but in her head. Silence filled her heart and she opened her mouth to shriek, but could not even hear herself. No longer was her mother holding her like other children were being held by their mothers, running, dodging for safety, even though there was no place for refuge. She stood up to run but her legs froze once she was standing because she did not know which way to turn. She could have begged for blindness, but her eyes were kept forced open by the horrors that could only be the white man's hell the black cloths tried to teach them about. The smoke from burning teepees stung her eyes and she dared not blink.

Wild Wind wanted nothing more than to be lifted out of the noise and chaos when she felt her hair being pulled, her feet leaving the earth and landing heavily on the sweaty nape of a horse. Her arms and legs shot out in all directions, searching for purchase on anything solid, but at the same time she tried to free herself from the grasp of the white man riding the horse. He held her tight with his arm pinning her to himself, the fancy shinny buttons scratching at her bare skin. It seemed like hours that she rode like this, terrified and looking desperately for her mother or father, anyone that she might recognize, but the wounds and the blood disguised everyone she saw.

Whether it was due to fear or shock, she had allowed herself to lean against the soldier, after what seemed like ages of struggling. When she was handed down to another set of white hands she shivered uncontrollably as the chill hit the side of her body that had grown warm against the soldier. They took her into the building where other white men dressed like him spoke noisily to each other with words she did not understand. The smells from their bodies and their food made her stomach knot tightly, as if it would keep her body from becoming tainted and making it sick.

It did not matter when they took turns poking and grabbing at her, spitting on her and distinctly laughing about her, even though she did not know their jokes. Wild Wind only knew she had to find her family and she blocked out any thoughts that any of them were at the mercy of white hands like she was. She would not risk even the thoughts of their demise. She concentrated on escape and plotted her vengeance against these white men who made her captive in person only, her spirit she let soar through the squares cut into the sides of the walls where she watched the warm reds and pinks of the sun set on the cold winter prairie.

Dog Days of Summer

The official start of summer was usually the second week of June. School was over for Anna and her older brother, Nick, with the weeks spread out in front of them like lazy dogs splayed out on the porch sunning. In the early hours of the morning, their mother would wake them up to go through the motions of putting on clothes and running a toothbrush across a few willing teeth.

They would leave their apartment above the drug store when the smell of morning from the café had started to waft through town. Still groggy from the vestiges of sleep, Anna would hug up close to the window as she rode behind her mother. She shivered with her bare skin touching against the vinyl seats of the car. Often the fog would lie across the curvy roads where there were low spots. It made Anna feel gloomy as she thought about the warm bed she had left, but her spirits lifted as the sun burned through the gauzy mist of the night.

At the farm, yellow spilled out of the kitchen window. Usually a pot of cornmeal mush bubbled slowly on the stove waiting for them. Scrambled eggs or pancakes were a treat which Grandmother rarely afforded. It was okay to Anna, as she usually sleep-walked through the chewing.

"Get in the house," their mother instructed from behind the wheel of the car. She had not bothered to get out of the car, much less putting it in park, only having time to press her foot hard on the brake pedal as Anna and Nick got out. "I'm already late."

Anna was obedient, until she thought she heard something whimpering, crying out in the front bushes. Nick poked at her as they headed towards the back door and said "you're hearing things."

After breakfast and chores, the morning dew had disappeared and Anna was headed to the grassy patch out front to play, when she remembered hearing sounds from the bushes. She was carefully exploring the edges of the bushes when she heard the whimpers again. Honing in on the source of the sound, Anna jumped back at the shiny orbs that looked out from a pile of fur. She sped to the back of the house where Poppa was sharpening the blade of a hoe.

"Poppa, there's something out in the bushes. There's an animal."

He followed her back and parted the bushes where Anna pointed. Nick's attention had been caught and tried to look past Poppa, forcing Anna to the other side of him.

"Hey, little fella," Poppa cradled a handful of fur and held it out for Anna and Nick to see.

"It's a puppy," Nick said, trying to touch its matted fur.

"What's wrong with his ear?" Anna pointed to his left ear that stood straight up in a jagged crop while the other tip drooped.

"Looks like he got into a fight." Poppa grabbed the pup's muzzle to examine the large scratch on its nose.

"Is he lost?" Anna asked.

"He ain't lost, you dummy," Nick informed Anna.

"He's too little to be away from his mother," Grandfather cooed softly and held the trembling fur against him as he walked towards the back of the house. "He's not lost anymore."

"What is that?" Grandmother asked, none too pleased. "Don't bring that dirty thing into my kitchen."

Poppa ignored her. "Anna, get a clean rag and your Grandmother's witch hazel."

"I'm sure you're bringing rabies and fleas into the house with that mongrel."

"We'll get him fixed up first and then he can go back outside," he reassured her.

"What kind of dog is he?" Nick asked as Poppa dabbed the wounds clean.

"Dunno. Probably won't know better until he grows up. Pretty sure he's a mutt. Heinz fifty-seven."

"That's catsup," Anna laughed.

Poppa was able to convince Grandmother to part with a slice of bread and some milk which he mushed up in a bowl and made a clumpy paste on his finger. He held it to the puppy's face. After an obligatory sniff, he licked Poppa's finger clean.

Nick took it upon himself to name the dog, Heinz, despite Grandmother's grumbling that the dog would bother her chickens and dig in the garden. "You need to do something about that dog," she would tell Poppa. He never looked her in the eye when he replied with a mumbled "uh-huh."

The summer passed with Anna and Nick spending their free time playing with Heinz. His ear healed, but he still looked funny with one ear always at attention and the other flopped over. Heinz had grown out of his puppy size but still wanted to play tug with sticks out in the yard. Anna and Nick tried to teach him to fetch the sticks, but he preferred to have games of tug-o-war.

By the next summer, Heinz was pretty much full grown. The black patches had spread apart some, on the buff background, giving him markings similar to a German Sheppard. But the floppy ears, actually only one, Poppa could only guess to its origin. "Loyalty is one of the most important virtues," Poppa would muse as he scratched Heinz behind his floppy ear. "It's a quality of great worth if you can get it in a man or dog."

Whenever Anna played on the grassy patch in the front yard, Heinz stationed himself between her and the road. Maybe only two or three cars would pass by while she was out playing, but he would lift his head as soon as he heard the sound and watch, not putting his head back down until the vehicle had disappeared from sight.

When cars or trucks would turn onto the drive, Heinz would jump up and bark. His tail wagged, kind of like Poppa waving his arm up high in greeting if he were off in the distance. People who were not dog people did not notice the wagging tail and would be intimidated by the bark. But even for people who knew Heinz, his sniffing was, for some, very embarrassing. Everyone got a thorough sniffing where they would have to push his snout away, otherwise trip, trying to walk with a dog muzzle between their legs.

Poor Millie O'Henry. Anna watched Heinz bury his nose between her legs as she teetered towards the house with a cake held high over her head, away from his slobbery canines.

"Nick," Grandmother yelled out the window. "Get that dog away from Mrs. O'Henry. Now."

Nick got up and ambled over sheepishly with his arms dangling side to side with each step. He knew he was going to have to grab Heinz by the scruff and pull him away, all too close to a vicinity on Mrs. O'Henry that he did not want to get near.

Anna was sure Heinz was smiling when he resumed his spot between her and the road. She wondered if he had found it humorous to embarrass Mrs. O'Henry or Nick.

Nick had decided to relax himself sprawled across the grass patch. Anna sat on a spot that his gangly arms or legs had not crowded out. They talked about school starting the next week. It was hot out and the thought of being cooped up in a classroom made them sweat. Even Heinz laid in the shade as still as possible, hoping for a stiff breeze to fill the yard.

Anna watched the heat wavering under the hazy sky and wistfully thought about how welcome a clap of thunder would sound, bringing with it the pelting rain and gusts of wind to sweep away the dustiness. Maybe even some hail stones. The sound on the roof and windows was scary and Grandmother would fret about the damage hail could do. It was such a treat if the pellets were big enough not to melt away before Anna and Nick could pop some of the icy coldness into their mouths. Poppa already said there was not any rain projected, when Grandmother had uttered her parched wishes for rain before the crops withered to nothing.

Anna lazily watched a stick wiggle at the side of the drive. By the time she realized what it was, Heinz had jumped up and grabbed it between his teeth. Nick ran over and encouraged the dog.

"Get it boy," he yelled and whooped. Anna felt anguish and fear surge through her. It was not because she was scared of the snake, but the way Heinz shook his head violently, snapping the ends of the garter from side to side. She could not hear the hisses as the black tongue flicked in and out over the dog's throaty growl.

"Anna! No!" she heard Poppa shouting. She looked at her hand holding a stick and she was hitting Heinz on the back with it. "Anna, he'll bite you."

Heinz started running towards the barn and Nick ran after him. Poppa bent down and grabbled Anna in his arms. She realized she was shaking against his solid body. She started crying and let herself melt in the safety of her grandfather's arms.

"It's okay. It's okay," he kept repeating against her sobs, until she caught her breath and started hiccupping. "I didn't want him to bite you. You shouldn't hit a dog."

"I'm," she hiccupped again. "I'm sorry."

"Are you okay?"

"Uh-huh," she rubbed her eyes. "Poppa. He was hurting that snake."

"I know. That's part of nature."

"You don't understand. The snake told me, but he didn't say any words." She watched Poppa stare into her eyes. It was less of him looking, trying to find something in her eyes as much as it felt like he was trying to show her things in his. She looked at his face and saw several different faces. They waivered back and forth like she had become dizzy, but her vision was steady as she absorbed the faces, none that she knew, but yet they seemed familiar. She saw the flames of a fire and an eagle spreading its wings against the blue sky and water flowing along creek banks. She blinked and saw the tears falling from his blue eyes and filling the wrinkles that ran down his tanned cheeks.

"The animals do speak," he affirmed. "They do speak. Not everyone can hear them."

"Can you?"

"Yes."

"Can Grandmother?"

"No."

"Can Momma?"

"No."

"Can Nick?"

"No."

"How come they can't?"

"Because your spirit has ears."

Anna was sure Poppa could hear her silent thoughts too, when he said, "Don't tell Grandmother. Don't tell the others who can't hear the animals. It would make them feel bad."

"Our secret?"

"Yes. Our secret. Let's go see what Nick is up to." Anna followed her grandfather, holding his hand, feeling the intimacy between their clasped hands.

Diagnosis

Everything I had done in the last two weeks had a new bitter flavor. So few times have I immediately known the end of one thing and a beginning of another, knowing the way I lived the rest of my life was forever changed. The birth of a first child is a defining moment, where everything before is childless and everything after is about that child. But usually there is a period of nine months, depending on the level of acceptance or denial, to get use to the idea of becoming a parent.

Usually the beginning and an end of a stage in life is gradual and is a thing only seen clearly, as clearly as it ever will be, from the back end, after the fact. But explaining the cancer diagnosis as having a bitter flavor is too generous, too strong when everything I did was with numbness in my mind. It had become a defining part of me but that too felt mostly make-believe, absurd.

After filling up the car, I screwed the gas cap back on and headed inside to pay, get some coffee and say hi to Theresa, if she was working. Selfishly I wanted to tell Theresa about the cancer diagnosis. I didn't want to make Theresa feel bad, like she had to offer condolences when she might not know what to say, but she always seemed to put things into perspective. I wondered how I should drop the bomb. I did not want to blurt it out like I was fishing for sympathy or pity.

As I started including cancer into my life, I contemplated war with it, a bare-handed battle. If the cancer was stronger than me and I lost, I knew what that would mean. I might not see my daughter give birth to her baby that was on its way and watch my other grandchildren grow up. I would not plant my garden next spring and sprinkle a bit of tobacco into the soil, offering it to Mother Earth, like I had seen Poppa do so many times. So much of what he taught me I had made a part of my life.

When Poppa died, I took his pouch of tobacco and hid it among my things. It lasted several years with only a pinch a year being used whenever I had a chance to plant a garden. I was still using the packet I had bought several years ago. Memories like that would not exist anymore. I was defeated by the thought of cancer and there was so much I needed to teach my children. And then I remembered what Poppa use to say, "You are part of the circle of life. Do you know what that means?"

"We are born and we give birth?" I had answered him so innocently, back as a child.

"Yes, that's part of it. But there's another part. Do you know what that might be?"

"No."

"We die and give life to other things."

I had understood Poppa to mean a person would know what they were giving life to before they died. It was so wrong, incorrect, an assumption of childlike thinking, like what he said was supposed to be comforting, not necessarily a painful truth.

Seeing Theresa counting packs of cigarettes, I waved to her as I got coffee.

"How you been, Anna?" Theresa greeted me, setting her clipboard down to take my money.

"Getting older and still broke." I chuckled, hoping to hide the nervous anticipation of wanting to tell Theresa about the diagnosis.

"Have a new collection for Blake Smith," Theresa said as she handed me my change and then pointed at the plastic jug on the counter. "You remember his daddy, Dale? Blake's his son. Got cancer, you know."

"No, I didn't." The confusion was not just remembering who Dale Smith was, but a new realization that we now had another connection besides growing up in the same town.

"He's got four little kids."

"Terrible."

"He lost his insurance too."

"What's he gonna do?"

"Dunno. The VFW's holding a spaghetti supper later this month."

"Best of luck paying those bills that'll probably outlast him," I said, trying to anesthetize and beat down my feelings by immersing myself in someone else's problems.

"Now a-days you got a fighting chance to beat cancer, but not if you don't have insurance."

The coins in the jug applaud as my handful of change joined them. The bell on the door rang as

41

another customer entered. A regular homecoming, it was Bobby Maxwell, a womanizing fixture of the community.

"We gotta do something about health care for people who don't have it," Theresa continued.

"Com'mon Theresa," he said pouring himself a cup of coffee. "I'm sick of hearing about people belly achin' bout that. If they want insurance, they're gonna have to earn it like us honest folks. Go get a job, I say, like me and you get up every day and work. How many years you put in here?"

"Eighteen years. Show up every day with a smile on my face and what do I get? Couple dollars above minimum wage and a chance to converse with witless wonders like you."

"I may be dumb, but I work for everything I get. Nobody giving me handouts. We earn ours, they can too if they really want it." He handed her a few crumpled up dollar bills from his pocket to pay for his coffee and the doughnut he had balanced on the lid of his cup.

"Get out of my store," Theresa laughed and did not even hand him his change but put it in the jug. "If there's anything left over from this, I'm gonna buy myself some insurance."

"Aw, Theresa. You're married. You're hubby takes care of that."

"And when he loses his job?"

I watched Theresa's forehead furrow in frustration as she started wiping down the counter in front of her, vigorously, like it was filthy. "Other girl who works here nights, she don't have no hubby, so she don't have insurance either. Thank goodness her kid's got Medicaid."

"Proves my point. If she were living right, she wouldn't have to worry 'bout things like that."

"You keep livin' right, you're not gonna need to worry about health insurance." She pointed her rag at his belly.

"God, I have yet to meet a woman who isn't a nag," he acted like he was pissed and winked at me.

The door bell rang as he left and Theresa sighed with frustrated anger. "I get so sick of people running their mouths like they know what they're talking about."

I just nodded my head.

"He'd be the first to bitch because he got shitty service filling his gas tank up. People like him expect the waitress at the restaurant to serve him and clean his dirty dishes and the grocery store clerk to make sure she rings up his case of beer correctly. There's plenty of us who work our asses off and he thinks we don't deserve health care to keep us healthy so we can keep putting food on our table."

I stood there, unable to find anything to add to or dispute to what she said, so I stood there sipping my coffee like it had purpose, as if it was the most important thing on my mind.

"What's going on with you?" Theresa asked, not in the casual tone of how people use it as a greeting, but as a question, an interrogation.

"Not much," I said hesitantly. "I don't know."

"I have this Wednesday off. You want to meet? We haven't talked in ages."

"Uh, yeah, sure if you want."

"You got something on your mind, I can see it in your eyes."

"Yeah. I got stuff, if you want to hear about it."

"Meet over at my house at ten, Wednesday and we'll do therapy."

And like a blessing, I had a new anxiety to worry about, scenarios to play out how I might tell her how my life had changed again. It was a great diversion to my real anxieties, kind of like when guests were expected and you found yourself sorting out the sock drawer when the rest of the house looked like hell's half acre. It would be just like Teresa to not even see the dirty dishes in the kitchen sink and say "get rid of the crap cluttering up your heart." My poor heart, it was so heavy and bulging out in all directions it was going to break. I know the cancer diagnosis was not all that was crammed in there. There was a bunch of other things in there, acting like those people who are loud and obnoxious, looking for attention and thought it was a party and decided to come uninvited.

The Way It's Done

"This is the way it's done," is how Grandmother explained the things she did. She crawled across the tilled soil to plant the delicate carrot seeds. Neat row after row is how Grandmother was sure a garden was grown. It was almost like going up and down the grocery store aisles when Grandmother went out into the garden with the splint-ash basket handle hanging from her arm. Anna learned to be careful and was allowed to help plant the peas and corn. She liked placing the hard kernels of corn and the dried peas with valleys of emptiness that would plump out into roots and leaves. In her mind's eye, she could taste the sweet bursts of tenderness that was created from the blossoms after the honeybees had tickled the bashful insides of the petals.

It was the dank of spring and Grandmother stood with her hands on her hips, mumbling where she should put the corn this year.

"Plant it with the peas and squash," Poppa said through the clenched teeth that held his sweet smelling pipe.

Grandmother harrumphed the idea. "That's not now we do it," she reprimanded when she could have just stated. Poppa tended the fields and the milk cow and the dozen or so sheep. Grandmother's domain was the house and the chicken coop and the vegetable garden.

Poppa looked sad and did not argue back. Anna sat down next to him in the grass. Grandmother was sometimes sharp with Poppa for no apparent reason. Anna wished he would stand up to her sometimes. But maybe in his own way he did.

Before Grandmother planted her garden she would ask Poppa if he got to tilling it.

"Yes, ma'am."

"And did you spread manure on it real well?"

"Yes, ma'am."

"Not the stuff from Hudson's you got for the field. I want the stuff from our animals on the garden."

"That's the stuff I used," he said to Grandmother and winked at Anna. "It's all shit."

"Thomas, you watch your mouth."

But Poppa never told Grandmother he had stopped the tractor while plowing and took a couple of pinches out of his pipe tobacco and sprinkled it in the moist dirt. Anna had watched him do this when she had been playing in the yard. She could see his lips moving as he patted the ground with his hands. His head jerked around and caught her staring. He smiled and got back on the tractor. Poppa did a lot of odd things, but she dared not question it in front of Grandmother, because she would just ridicule him. If she could protect Poppa from Grandmother, she would. Anna was pretty sure that was loyalty, like he spoke of Heinz.

In the late summer before school started, Anna

would help Grandmother cart in pail after pail of tomatoes into the kitchen. Into the big white enamel pot with black trim, Grandmother would first boil the water and put a batch of tomatoes into the hot water and then scoop them out for a cold water bath in a pan already set up in the sink. The translucent skins would then be peeled off. Anna would sneak a strip of tomato skin and stick it on her arm, pretending it was her own. It was not as fun as peaches, where Grandmother would set the waste bowl, full of pits and peach skins on the kitchen table and Anna and her brother were allowed to eat all the skins they wanted.

Anna and Nick were not allowed near the stove as Grandmother moved too fast and a child in the way could trip her up, she said. She and Nick would sit with Poppa at the kitchen table until called to the sink to help. Cutting a tomato in half, he tilted it towards Anna.

"Count the seeds, Anna. How many are there?" he asked, pointing to the juicy flesh with the tip of the knife. "Each one can grow and make a new plant."

"That's a lot of plants."

"That's how seeds are collected and dried for the next season."

"How come you and Grandmother don't do that?"

"No thanks. I'll order mine," Grandmother snorted. "Quit putting ideas in her head."

The sound of the back door slapping shut made Anna look up to see Nick grabbing at Heniz who took the opportunity of an opening door to come see what was going on.

"Get that dog out of the house," Grandmother yelled. "How many times do I have to tell you that? I swear you children would be just as happy running around like a bunch of savages."

"That's not a word I want to hear you calling them," Poppa had said in a quiet voice, but with the power of the low rumble of thunder off in the distance.

Anna looked up to see Poppa standing up. The kitchen was quiet except for the water bubbling the canning jars against the sides of the pot. Heinz stopped his panting and lowered his ears flat against his head, barely daring to look at Poppa.

"You define a child like that, it will keep them in that place forever," Poppa took Nick's arm in one hand and Anna in the other. "I prefer to call them precious." He went out the back door with Nick and Anna following, even Heinz didn't need coaxing, but not before Grandmother gave a final harrumph as the door closed behind them.

Each fall Bob and Jake would come and help Poppa with harvest. Their laughing and joking was delicious to hear and Anna would stealthily incorporate herself in their space. Jake would wink at her whenever Bob started clowning.

"Anna, you get in the house," Momma yelled out the back door. Anna dragged her feet and wished her mother was more like Poppa instead of Grandmother. The screen door had yet to slam shut behind her when her mother's hand met her behind. "You stay away from them. Those niggers are for working, not for having fun," she had said none too quietly and her voice easily carried out into the yard.

After that Anna did notice Bob and Jake would hang their heads and wipe the smiles off their faces and mumble "yes ma'am" and "no sir" whenever Momma was present or another neighbor was at the farm.

Anna made sure that Momma wasn't around when she decided to defy her. Grandmother was surprisingly indifferent to Bob and Jake when they came up to the house to wash up and eat the lunch she had prepared for them. On those days, it was a picnic held outside the kitchen door for everyone on boards that were lined up to make a table and benches to sit on.

In the dead of winter, Grandmother would announce chicken coop cleaning. It was on a sunny day and reasonably warm out, but it was still winter as snow was usually on the ground. She would enlist Anna and Nick and her cousins to help clean out the coop, scrub it down with bleach and then white-wash the walls and put down new bedding.

After the hen house was put back in order, Grandmother would bathe the children. The girls first and then the boys. The boys were more resistant to Grandmother's thoroughness in scrubbing. In a tub full of boys, Nick could be heard yelling "leave some skin, would ya?" The sound of wet flesh being smacked could be heard. Grandmother's hand print could be seen on Nick's face after the bath.

Everyone lined up in the kitchen and waited their turn to get their heads oiled. It was smelly and sticky, but Anna liked the way her hair shined the next day when the oil would be washed out.

Grandmother was one not to mess around and joke. She felt everything one did must be taken seriously and she always linked it to affecting money, whether it was being made or wasted. She was always in motion and it was always fast and deliberate, perhaps to make time for the periodic thumps on the head or slaps she handed out wherever she saw fit. There was never any middle ground with Grandmother.

Poppa was different than Grandmother. Anna knew the touch of his hands against her own skin well. Always gentle. Even with the boys, he was gentle. Where Grandmother used fear to make the kids behave her, the kids behaved Poppa, fear of letting him down. One did not fear letting Grandmother down, you just feared her.

Momma would make fun of Grandmother sometimes, but always when she was at least a mile out of earshot. Even joking about Grandmother was more serious than funny. It took Anna a while to understand when her mother said grey was not a color Grandmother believed in.

Momma said Grandmother's hair was chestnut brown, that glossy brown that is not so dark it absorbs all the light that hits it, or so fair like a varnished pine board that reflects a glare. It was the medium brown that holds the light a little longer, where the light lingers before it comes back to you as glowing. Grandmother's hair went from chestnut brown to white in a blink of an eye. Anna had not witnessed it, but tried to believe what her mother said. No grey to introduce white, as if her hair was just Grandmother's personality coming out. Grandmother was so old that Anna could not imagine her as once young.

Grandmother had yet to kill Anna or her brother or her cousins, but her ability and right to do it was a sense of fear they all carried. Grandmother did not seem to distinguish between respect and obedience, as long as her grandchildren gave it. "Yes ma'am, no ma'am," and "Grandmother" when she was being soft. No Granny or Gram for her. She was Grandmother and that is what she needed to be referred to as. Coming under Grandmother's evil eye could turn one's bones to jelly. The caustic properties of her voice would burn welts onto one's soul.

Only Poppa seemed to have any control over her. Not necessarily control, but he knew how to encourage her kindness to come out of hiding. He loved her and it was hard to understand loving any person in this way. The grandchildren loved her like they loved the Lord, with fire in one hand and brimstone in the other.

For Grandmother's birthday the next summer, Poppa got Anna's mother to bake a cake. Uncle Wes and the cousins arrived promptly at three in the afternoon. Grandmother pshawed the idea of celebrating an adult's birthday as silly, childish. But when Poppa presented her with the rose-peony bush, she was tight lipped and the muscles could be seen flexing in her jaw. She willed a collection of accumulated tears to stay in her eyes.

"That's too much money to waste on my birthday," she finally spoke.

"For you, it's not a waste," Poppa reassured. "It's a gift of love."

"You spoil me," she choked out through a smile, funny looking and out of place on Grandmother's face.

They planted it on the left-hand side of the front steps and it became Grandmother's pride and joy. It did not take too much imagination for Anna to believe that

Poppa and Grandmother were talking about her instead of a peony bush. She was pretty sure that each one of the grandkids were gifts of love in her grandparent's eyes, even when Grandmother was passing out orders and thumps on the head. It was a feeling she could not imagine changing.

In the summertime, one could almost imagine Grandmother's temper warming the air. Most of her agitation came from her belief that weeds in her garden were evilness. It was Poppa who knew the names for all of them. Grandmother poo-pooed that as nonsense, kin to naming the livestock that would end up on a dinner plate. Poppa loved to tease her and say he had a taste for some dandelion greens or burdock. He seemed to be the only one un-phased by Grandmother's evil eye.

It was a blazing hot afternoon with the sun high overhead when Grandmother announced that Nick would hoe around the corn and Anna would weed the carrots in the garden. Anna begged to weed something else. She hated weeding the carrots. Their feathery tops where hard to discern from the grass that would grow in between them. One had to be careful with yanking the weed, else the thread-like root of the carrots would come clean out. There was no replanting the uprooted, they wilted before she finished a row and when Grandmother came to check how she did, she would swat Anna if too many had been killed.

"Let me switch with Nick," Anna begged, after Grandmother had issued orders at the kitchen table, as they finished lunch.

"No," both Grandmother and Nick replied.

"I don't want to do it. I'm not going to work in

the hot sun and work like a nigger."

Nick laughed until he saw Poppa's grave face. Anna looked at her grandfather and saw the hurt that began at his eyes and radiated out in each canyon of wrinkles traveling across his face. It was not what she expected. Anger maybe. Amusement perhaps, but not sadness and hurt.

Grandmother stared at Poppa, her lips tight and hands clasped in front of her, uncharacteristically quiet and still. Poppa cleared his throat.

"Anna," he said with a coldness Anna had never experienced from him before. "That is very disrespectful."

"I'm sorry," she muttered in the smallest voice as she hung her head.

"Do you even know who you're being disrespectful to?"

"You and Grandmother?"

"No."

"No?"

"You're being disrespectful to anyone who isn't white."

"Okay."

"You never know who has roots that aren't white. You need to be careful. You..."

"Thomas, stop," Grandmother interrupted. "You children listen to your grandfather. Don't say it again."

"Yes, ma'am," Anna and Nick both said.

Grandfather got up from the table and went outside. Anna noticed his broad shoulders did not echo the straight sharp corners of the door frame like they usually did. His shoulders slumped as he let the screen door slap closed behind him.

Winners of the West

After being weaned on the deaths of her loved ones, she was still unprepared for the murder of her husband. Sadly, I watched as she held their sons, like she was afraid they might dissolve between her arms she wrapped around them so tightly, refusing to let go when they squirmed. Somewhere in the embrace, I imagined she could only hope to feel her husband, a selfish wish she could not extend to the others who also mourned his death.

Her husband had always been a quiet boy, obedient to a fault to his mother and then to her, the girl named Never Tamed, he became her quiet protector. The Quiet One took much teasing from the other full bloods his age that he was too weak to be a warrior and would be a woman in any marriage. But those same boy's fathers said that about me too, his father, Patrick, Sky Lives In His Eyes. I was quiet and respectful of my wife and didn't need to be boisterous and insult her to show them how I was in charge. A half-blood, I was, but neither the white nor the red blood in me could understand belonging to something in the way of being owned. I could hardly own someone feeling this way. I was proud of my son, living as what I saw as noble by treating his wife the same as he saw me treat his mother.

The little girl who came to us from the first bitter winter winds in the west, we named Never Tamed because she would never willingly give admittance of being owned. If she belonged to something it was because she wanted it, but would never be owned by it. And no one would understand her or be able to console her, even in the last few hours of her life.

She came to us from the most unlikely place. A white man stiff in his cavalry uniform, had plucked her from the burned wreckage of her home, her family, her village. I remember how the soldier had an empty quality to his eyes. Perhaps they had not always been like that before the last days of 1890 in the Dakota Territories. It was the pale faces motive to break the Indians by never giving them good reason or peace. At least with this one white man, it had succeeded by haunting his spirit.

He had been a privileged officer of the Civil War and had lived it unscathed and untouched, something an Indian would consider a coward to go into battle and not leave even a drop of his own blood on the ground. Being sent to the reservation office at Rosebud was quite possibly his first interaction with the enemy, seeing their eyes up close enough to tell what color their eyes were, and what it was like to live because you killed someone who would have done the same to him. But for all the bravado in his voice when he talked about being in the military before the Wounded Knee massacre, it was apparent that he never thought of women and children being war casualties of his own hands.

Of all the meetings with the Indian Agents and the Indian Chiefs and the interpreters, there was always a subtlety in language that was misconstrued by one or the other. Listening to any of them was always subject to hearing the lies woven tightly with the truths, always doubting what one was really hearing. But it was that little girl, who the soldier thought he understood completely, when she sounded as his own little girl had. If he had not turned around to look, he would have always, despite the absurdity, wondered if it was his little girl he heard screaming.

Under his direction were seasoned soldiers who took it upon themselves to teach the new recruits on the savagery of Sitting Bull and his Sioux warriors who desecrated the bodies of Lt. Col. Custer and his men. The Great Father in Washington decided that the Indians would be brought into the reservation if they would not voluntarily come themselves. With the Minneconju Chief, Big Foot, on the move with his band, the U.S. Army Commanding Officer Colonel Forsyth and Agency Commander Major General Brooke voiced fears of the Indian's devilry could very well mimic Little Big Horn. The savages had to be eradicated for the safety of the civilized. They were dangerous. Even when giving them the gift of their own land in the form of reservations, the soldiers knew the Indians were always complaining, never grateful, and lazy, all the bragging of their ferocious warriors only to be mush-mouthed cry babies and unwilling to take a spade to the earth for their own survival.

Any interaction with the Indians required the soldiers to be on their guard and react quickly to orders given. The feeling may have been his own, but preceding the meeting to have the Lakota give up their arms, was heavy with apprehension. He explained that quite likely it was anxiety of the Anglo Christmas holiday being only days past and the bitter cold of winter perhaps warmer than the feelings of most of the men being away from loved ones on such a sacred holiday. The apprehension of the New Year approaching could have added to it too. He refused to pass judgment on his fellow soldiers and contradict what the government had decided and declared what happened at the Wounded Knee Creek.

The soldier related that he was hoping for a relatively uneventful morning while they collected guns and weapons from the Indians, selfishly hoping to make it back early so he might rest himself from a sickness that had made its rounds through the rank of soldiers. He recalled being careful not to accidently bump into any of the men, as if it might set them off, as they were ridged in body and mind, ready to jump to action like a tightly coiled spring. The Indians were instructed to place their weapons in a pile. His fellow soldiers glared at them with suspicion while the Indians refused to look at the soldiers as they lay their weapons down, only daring to sneak looks after they rejoined their group. It was a pitiful amount of guns and ammunition that was given up and it was ordered that each Indian was to be searched. One of the young Indian men started waving his gun in the air and started yelling in a slurred speech which everyone understood him to be dumb, more so when he disregarded orders from the soldiers and even his own fellow Indians like he was deaf to reason. Later in the government inquires it was rumored that this Indian, Black Coyote suffered deafness. The soldier said he personally did not know, only recalled the Indian waving his arms above his head in a threatening way, but as untrustworthy as the Indians were and him being a proud military man, did not necessarily wish to commit this as a fact, by doing so, would make the United States soldiers at fault. But if the soldiers felt threatened, their fault was defending themselves. A shot was fired, many of the soldiers afterwards reported it came from the Indian's gun as soldiers struggled with him to release the gun. Immediately, gunfire could be heard from the carbines and then the Hotchkiss guns positioned up on the surrounding hills broke through the screams and war whoops from the Indians.

Known as the Battle of Wounded Knee, the U.S. Army had crushed the Indians in the massacre. Some of the soldiers were blamed for killing women and children, but their justification was the squaws and children were equally dangerous and showed no respect to white authority. At least this is the answer that the pale faces are willing to give for the question of why. And I dare to guess Black Coyote, speaking with his hands, was asking the same thing with his arm waving above his head, why did he have to give up his gun?

It had all started with what the pale faces called our 'Messiah Craze,' calling it that with ridicule in their speech, cutting us down as a race when we, tired and broken grasped at salvation, wanting safety for our spirits, hope for our lands returned, our enemies smitten. We wanted it for our children and vindication of our dead. It was a prophesy of the buffalo returning that was down-right lunacy in the eyes of those who believed in Manifest Destiny, arrogantly laying claim to this land that would would flow with milk and honey.

And our adopted daughter, Never Tamed, had belonged to a tribe that had been indoctrinated by the Ghost Dance, the hope for Indian salvation in the midst of white persecution. The whites gave us Christianity and when we attempted to incorporate pieces into our culture, it resulted in apocalyptic results. She was apparently the only thing that soldier came across that was still intact. A part of his heart had softened at the idea she was as innocent, fragile as any baby animal. Her wild eyes peered around suspiciously and seemed to contradict her tininess. Being little and cute, he undoubtedly figured she could hardly muster enough strength to hurt anything. He related this story to me and alluded to his fellow officers ranging in affections towards her as something to be pitied to something they could carry out their perversions with bald-faced violence. But she became something he had to protect, and after a few days it was a nuisance, a liability. More work than he was willing to do for a souvenir of her people's defeat.

He told me this as I invited him into my home and watched his appraising eyes scan what I had graciously offered him for a meal. He ate the food with what others might have called politeness, forcing his teeth to mash the food enough to swallow with hard, forcible gulps. I pitied this man, having to eat his food seasoned with suspicion. Regardless of who we were, we were considered savages and renegades. Having our likeness stamped on buttons or medals to hang on their military uniforms was no less a mark of pride for themselves, as if they could be wearing a scalp or had whittled a notch into their weapon, bragging not just "the only good Indian is a dead Indian," but they had accomplished just that.

This man was the weakest kind. He knew what was right, something the white's tried to explain as Christianity even though we knew it as respect, but yet he was unable to follow through, stand up for what he knew was right. He was relieved to give this child to someone who might allow her to belong. He explained that he knew what it was like for a wild animal to be caged up, away from its own kind, and how it became an empty shell, dangerous when all it could fill it with was anger and fear. He also knew the danger she would be in if she were to stay among the white men.

The White Man was sure he was leaving her with her own kind. But she was Sioux, plains people, only because my ancestors drove them out of the forests of the Mississippi headwaters before they called the land surrounding the Missouri River home, when the Whites drove my people westward. What he may have not known in his generalization was how we coveted our children. Children period, they are precious, they are the future, the continuation of life when we die. To not treat this child as most precious would have been shameful in the eyes of any Indian. That was one thing common between our tribe and hers, beyond that, we could not even speak each other's languages. I could not raise her as a Teton Sioux, but would raise her as a Ojibwe, hoping for her to find her place in that society and feel a part of something again when everything she knew had been taken away. That is how the name she knew herself as Wild Wind was changed to Never Tamed.

Your Real Parents

Anna liked to tag along behind Grandfather on lazy Sunday afternoons after dinner. Grandmother would sit in her rocker with her knitting, but really it was a chance for her to take a nap. Momma would paint her fingernails or read a romance novel. Anna and her brother would be shoed out of the house on account of making too much noise. Usually Grandfather would ask if Anna and Nick wanted to go for a walk to the woods.

It was fall and the leaves gave off a spicy smell, along with all the stuff the summer heat had baked. It was like dessert to the nose, especially after the dinner of chicken and thick gravy over mashed potatoes. That nice kind of filling food, where it felt good to fill even the tiniest cracks of one's appetite, after a summer of fresh vegetables. The fresh garden bounty was good, especially after going without all winter and spring and Anna could not wait to sink her teeth into a buttery ear of corn or hear the snap of cucumber between her teeth. But by fall, she wanted something rich and filling.

Grandmother would declare "you kids are either growing or getting ready to hibernate," when Anna and her brother held their plates up for second helpings.

Grandmother had made a great lemon pie, with light as air meringue on top, but Anna was ready to trade it in for a heavy piece of pumpkin pie.

Nick decided to read a comic book under the oak tree and went to flop down on the green carpet of fine bladed grass with a Coke. Anna toted her Coke and sipped on it every few steps. Sometimes she and Poppa would talk quite a bit on the walks, but usually he was quiet, perhaps absorbing the tranquility of the changing season. She looked down to see what he was looking at, or up in the sky, or out in the distance, trying to see what held his interest so intently.

They walked along the edge of the cornfield and neared the edge of the swail when Anna had finished her soda. She cocked her arm back, like her brother had shown her how to throw a baseball, and the bottle soared through the air and faintly could be heard to plop somewhere in the middle of the mess of brush.

"Anna," Poppa shouted at her and lumbered towards her. She felt him grab her by the arms, his grip tight, hurting her as he squeezed the flesh tight against the bone. Her mouth opened to cry out in pain, but she was so shocked at him, no sound came out. Never in her memory, had she heard him speak so angrily. He loosened his grip as he bent down in front of her.

"You can't do that," he said softly and with gentleness that contradicted the anger that was in his voice moments before.

"I'm sorry, Poppa."

"No. You don't understand," he sighed and stood up. "Come on." He offered her his hand. They started walking towards the woods.

"Everything you do, you do to Mother Earth."

Anna looked up to him quizzically, squinting in the sun and shading her eyes with her free hand.

"Anytime we throw our trash down we aren't respecting the earth. Every time I have to plow the fields I'm cutting away at Mother Earth's flesh. Every time I put chemicals on the field, I'm poisoning her." Tears overflowed his eyes. Anna knew his vision had to be wavering, mimicing what she heard in his voice.

"The swail doesn't sing anymore because the birds keep dying."

"How do you know this?"

"The Indians knew this, the natives of this land," his voice dropped in timbre as he swept his arm out in front of him. "They respected Mother Earth and whatever Father Sky gave them."

"But the Indians even believed people were created out of mud," she recalled being told that story at school when they studied Indians in history. She had laughed along with the other children and even the teacher, knowing all people had come from Adam and Eve.

Poppa cupped Anna's face with both of his hands and lifted her face up. "You're Indian, Anna." He stroked her hair out of her eyes. "You are Ojibwe. We are part of the Anishinaabeg people. You have Indian blood in your veins. Your mother does. Your brother does. I do."

"Does Grandmother?"

"No," Poppa became firm with his speech. "Grandmother does not and you do not need to remind her. Grandmother doesn't tolerate Indian ways, but she had her reasons."

"What's that?"

"She's afraid. She loves me and loves your mother and loves you and your brother, but knows how the white man's heart is against Indian blood."

"I'm not white?" Anna asked aloud, because she could not fathom that Poppa was not making this all up. How could she not be white with her red hair and blue eyes? Even Poppa's eyes were blue beneath his black hair.

"You are Indian. We believe our children are the future. Your Grandmother cherishes you as much as anyone could. She is protecting you and your brother and even your mother. You must help her protect everyone by not repeating this."

"Why are you telling me?" Anna asked in a begging tone, wondering if she wanted such responsibility.

"My parents and my grandparents and their parents and their parents can only be kept alive only if you know who you are. For me to stay alive, I need you and your children and their children, until you have great-great grandchildren to know."

"But how can I tell them if Grandmother can't know?"

"Because in your heart you know. With your heart you will teach your children what is right and to respect the earth and thank the sky for the privilege to wake up every day."

She grasped Poppa's hand tighter, willing to let him guide her safely through a new life he had awakened her to, because she did not know who she was anymore. It was full of new possibilities, but it broke everything she knew and believed up to that point into little bits. Like a mirror where she saw her reflection and it was broke, so now she saw herself in the broken fragments.

What did it mean to be white, Anna wondered. What did it mean to not be white. She knew how Poppa felt about what he was. Proud, but secretive. A contradiction with secrets usually meant guilt or shame. It was not like being secretive at Christmas and having a surprise of joy at the end. If Poppa's secret was opened where all could see, she knew it would end with bad things happening. But she was curious to know how Grandmother dealt with it.

"Grandmother," Anna asked while working on her homework. "What are we?"

"What are you talking about, child?"

"What ethnicity are we?"

"Why do you ask?" she asked almost accusingly. "Did someone say something?"

"We're not Irish or Italian. What are we?"

"Well," Grandmother stopped ironing on one of Poppa's shirts. "My parent's came from England. Your Poppa," she hesitated. "Was from Europe. Hungary or Lithuania."

"I thought someone said he was Spanish with the dark hair and blue eyes."

"Then why are you asking me these questions?" She resumed ironing, but with irritation in her voice. "Don't you have things to do? Did you finish weeding the carrots?"

Anna huffed and slid out of her chair and headed out the door, letting the screen door slap on the jamb. Grandmother was not being truthful and Anna believed there were other reasons she and Poppa wanted to keep who they were a secret.

By My Hands

The Anishinaabe Indians had hunted the swamps of the land of Michigamee, fished from its shores and created the lore and stories that explained the land they called home. We did not own it, and I tried to explain to white people who felt they could gain likeness with my whiteness. I asked them if they owned their mothers? Their fathers? Could they possibly own the people who gave life to them? No? Well, that is how we felt about Mother Earth and Father Sky and the Great Spirit.

For some reason when we admitted we did not own the land, the white man believed that they could take it for their own, possession without having to share. With discussion, we tried to convince the white man we would share it with them. But like a selfish child, it had to be theirs, making us constantly battle with these white men, generations of people from all the Indian Nations killed by generations of the white man's people who were arrogant with their thoughts and ideologies of civilization. Except for that last white generation, they decided that our last generations of Indians, worn tired from bullying, hungry for food we used to glean from the land with our own hands and starved on their commodities, weak from sickness that was beyond our medicine, the white man begrudgingly said we could hold land they did not want, we could own it, but would have to pay the Great Father money every few seasons. The Great Father would only accept the cold metal or the flimsy paper that would hardly make any warmth as fuel to a fire. In Indian society, if one wanted to give or receive something from another, it had to be something of use, such as meat from a deer, food for our bellies, hides for keeping us warm. And with our Great Spirit, we could give directly, a bit of tobacco. With the white's Great Father, we never gave directly. The men who collected for him, seemed to not be taken care of by the Great White Chief, for they requested more coins for their own troubles.

How were we to keep up with their requests? We didn't want to own our home, we just wanted to live there and let it take care of us while we took care of it in return. They called us savage and took away our abilities to provide for ourselves and then we froze and starved in the winters. How do you hunt the animals who still call the land home, smarter than the whites and even the Indians who came around to the idea of ownership? The *waabooz* and the deer could hardly know what ownership was and stay put. We were no longer able to follow the animals to feed our families. We were no longer able to travel north for the sweet berries, to the west for the fish and south for the willow. We had heard the stories of the plentitude of buffalo in the west, the tribes following the herds and taking what they needed until the next hunt. But the white man came and like a spoiled child, took more than he needed, wasted what he could not use, and was surprised when there was little left when he went back for more.

We could take the excess of our hunts and take them to the white man and turn it into the coins he requested as payment for land we knew we could not own. But confined to what they called reservations, we never had extra provisions to store for later, we never were able to even have what we needed. We had so little to glean from the land, within the boarders we were restricted to, we had to depend on meat that stank of improper care, or what a lazy person wouldn't do so their catch would spoil before it could be eaten. We had to depend on the sugar and flour that was always eventful when opening the bag for the first time and freeing the winged insects. We speculated that the white man could not be healthy if they had to depend on this kind of nourishment too.

They knew nothing, or refused to think about the taste of the land that seasoned the venison or berries or lake rice. In the deer you could taste the cedar swamps they called home. In the bright red *ode'iminan* you could taste how the sunshine flavored its flesh dimpled with gold. The tart of the sumac reminded us of the bitter cold that would come with the changing seasons and you could taste the sweetness of the delicate flesh of the fish who swam in the pure lake water.

We were cut off from the land where precious and important plants grew and we were unable to cure what ailed our health. In some cases, we could not even sneak on to land that was not our own and collect what we needed, for the plants had been destroyed by the plow that cut into the flesh of Mother Earth by the farmers or scraped away as the lumberjacks cut down the trees, dragged them across the earth, making it inhospitable for the mosses or mushrooms used for our survival.

We were able to trade animal pelts for coins that sang of cold promises. We became more like the white man when we scoured the land of anything that might be considered to have value, such as the fur of the animals. It was interesting, we Indians were trading away what we found precious, but basically worthless to the other. The whites took the skins of the animals and used them to trim their coats and hats. Decorations. How let down the animal would be to know their life was taken for the vanity of another. The coins were worthless to us, only helpful in purchasing white man products, and yes, purchase the use of land we still could not fathom owning, just incongruous, like the stars twinkling during the day, the sun too jealous to share the sky with anything else.

The whites irrationally cared about saving our heathen souls, teaching us what they thought were sins and what were not, like we were ill-equipped with knowing right from wrong. They cared about us as numbers, the rez agent counting heads, trying to record days of our birth and death, with little care for the days in between. The white man also tracked us with what they called a census. To us we knew it was another way to make our numbers put more money into their pockets, more land under their feet. The missionaries gave us Anglican names, ones that their God would recognize, and the census agents and the rez agents recorded them along with dates.

The churches kept sending missionaries to us natives. But they sent ministers to the whites. The missionary was synonymous, a symbol of savages, therefore keeping the 'savage' label clear in the minds of the whites. They wanted our children, promising to cleanse their souls, return them, clean and pure as the snow, shaming us that we had neglected our children, our future.

The whites thought Indians to be stupid, so they took advantage of us. There was no need to exercise their conscience with something less than human, us, the Indians, even though their missionaries thought they could beat a Christian conscience into the children at the Mission schools. Kick the dog while it was down. We knew it was only a person without a conscience who was capable of doing that.

The rules the whites laid out for admittance to their heaven and to their hell, made no sense to us. They told us it didn't matter what our hearts were, only if in our minds we believed their great spirit, Jesus, died for our sins, we would go to heaven. Natives who did not have a good heart were driven out of our communities, we could hardly care what they believed. It seemed a terrible contradiction.

They stuck with ten rules, mostly things we would not think of doing anyways in our culture. But maybe they had good reason, for the natives who drank the fire water started acting more like the white man, and started breaking those ten rules. As smart as their Great Spirit was, he had given them no rules on how he would like them to take care of the land and the water that he had given them as such a great gift.

When Never Tamed came to us, there was an uneasiness about her, like watching a tethered predator pace back and forth. But it was her own thoughts which haunted her spirit. Even in her sleep she would thrash and yell out to invisible captors. When she married the Quiet One, all were hopeful of her finding peace. They had two boys over the course of many moons and they grew bigger and bigger, yet Never Tamed and The Quiet One had less and less to give them. It made her swallow hard to decide to go into the white man's world voluntarily.

Never Tamed understood the contradictions of the white world and thought she was strong enough to enter their world and come out unscathed. Yet, she would not allow the misery of her childhood, when the white man entered her world, to let her believe she would come out any other way. To not consider everything before venturing out was reckless of her.

"I hear the howl of death in my ears from when I was a little girl. The white man took my family, took my life. They are greedy, they will take my boys by starving them because I cannot feed them from the land they tether me to. If the white man requests silver coins to rub between his fat fingers, we have to enter the white world and get those coins, if only to give them back. I have no pride when it comes to the boys, I will do what I have to so their bellies don't groan."

Never Tamed and The Quiet One made it into the white man's world and found work at the back of a butchers shop. He was to cut the animal up and she was to slice the meat into the chunks the shopkeeper had instructed her with.

They were told by the shopkeeper, "you steal a sliver of meat from me and that will be the last piece your whole family will ever chew." So she asked for skins and bones that were to be thrown away to fill a stew pot at her own home. They worked quietly and took their money at the end of each week to buy a little meat for the boys to make their bodies strong, the rest of the money was saved so they could pay the white man who collected for the Great Father and the boys would have a place to sleep every night. Going into the white town was like plunging into cold water, numbing them and taking more energy for them to stay alive than they could give.

The shopkeeper had left early one afternoon, and a group of men had formed. She informed them the shop was closed and they would have to come back the next day. They caught sight of the quiet man and demanded he open up, chided him to get his squaw to let them in.

"She said the store is closed." This garnered all kinds of taunts from the white men, asking him if he was so weak she was the boss.

"The store is closed." He repeated.

One of the white men barged in and commanded to his fellows, "I want to show this injun how to control his woman. You help him watch while I show him," with that, a few of the men grabbed the Quiet One while the white man grabbed the untamed woman and held her while she thrashed. "One of ya hold her arms, while I git her legs. She's all wild."

She howled at her assailants and she cursed the men with what she knew of white and Indian words.

People on the street could be seen stepping off the sidewalk and walking an arc around the store.

Instead of holding him to watch the taming of his wife, the white men pummeled him with their fists and got him to the floor where the ridged edges of their boots meet with the soft flesh of the Quiet One. It seemed hard for some of the men to not have a bit of the action, so they uncoordinatedly switched places.

She caught a glimpse of her husband and she knew his spirit had fled his body. All over her own body she felt the caustic burn like the sour taste when her body would purge itself of the contents of her belly. It was the memories of standing alone among her family, lying dead on the ground everywhere she looked. Her fear had been replaced with anger, fury, and this time she would not be helpless.

A blow to Never Tamed caused so much pain that had diminished her ability to fight back and she lay on the floor as the men started to lose interest in their prey. The one white man who seemed to be the last in their group, went back for the woman as the rest of them were filing out of the store. He was going to take his turn too, he yelled after them, Somehow Never Tamed had made it to her work station and held a butcher knife behind her back as he came to get her. As his arms grabbed her, she plunged the knife into his back. As he staggered back, she ran the knife into him again and again and again. He fell to the floor, laying in a pool of blood that grew wider around him.

She justified the blood on her hands, even if it was a white man's blood. In her culture, men who took advantage of the women and hurt them, were not allowed the benefit of banishment, but were taken away from the tribe and returned to the earth. An eye for an eye, the men dressed in black cloth had quoted from the Bible. What she did was not very different from their book of instructions.

I told her, "No, that is not how they will see it. The score is not even now, they will take revenge next, not your life but your sons." She balled her fists up as she listened to me after she had stolen a horse to bring her husband's body back home.

"Are they innocent and to be punished because of my actions, the same actions any woman would do if she watched her husband kicked to death after watching his wife being violated like I have? I am surely dead for all times if they are killed like me instead of making their own families when they are men."

"I will protect them, but you will have to let me."

"But for my sons, I will take whatever punishment I am given, I will do anything to know I can touch their faces and know they are alright."

"I will take care of them. I will not allow them to be tormented by these white men here. I have considered you my daughter from the day I took you from that white man. I still consider you that. Because it is more important for me to protect you from the white man, I must do what makes my heart heavy. They will not punish you for killing a white man. No, they will do worse, and because you are female, they will do worse to you than if you were a man. When they are done with you, you will be dead on the inside but your outsides will be as empty as a tree that stands, but all the heartwood is rotted out, leaving only a home for bad spirits. If they kill you while they do worse to you, or when you do succumb to death, you will take all of that evilness with you and forever wander the earth, never finding peace as you beg to haunt those who will have forgotten all about you."

I explained how we would protect her sons, my grandsons. I explained that it was as much my responsibility as it was hers to carry out this plan for the preservation of the boys' lives. When neither of us were no longer in this world in our current appearance, we would still be here in the form of the boys decedents.

We understood the wielding of power from the white men. For any of us to expect mercy or respect from them was something false. We found it noble of our men to fight to the death if it required. If a white man was killed, it was a shame, slaughtered in the hands of a savage. They had been taking our women who were unwilling for hundreds of years. They entered our women uninvited and ransacked their minds. Half-breeds were all around us, yet, when the white man looked at a half-breed all they saw was the Indian, tainting all the white, and that part was dead in their eyes. Regardless of being half white and half red, the whites felt they never could accept the shadowlanders as if tainted. I prefer to think of it as the red is so much stronger than the white, blanc, as the French taught us, blank, we thought they were saying when we mistakenly confused the English and French languages.

"Your days of happiness are over," I held her face, making sure that she saw into my eyes, my sincerity and my love for her, my dead son, and his innocent sons. "By my hands, I want this to be the worst you take with you into death."

We took the boys to the Catholic Priest at the church, thinking they might be safest with their white hands protecting them from those wanting revenge. Only after we begged him to keep them safe, we started out for the forest to find a place in the forest where her heart could feel calm and we would be undisturbed for the time we needed for our purpose. I built a fire for her to burn the sweet grass, cedar and sage to purify her body while she sang her death song to let Mother Earth and Father Sky that she would soon be leaving the earth and to let her ancestors know she was coming to join them. I went off in the distance, back towards the village, in case the whites had organized and were coming for her. I polished the gun carefully, wanting to make sure it would work the first time I squeezed the trigger. I prayed over the bullet I loaded, asking it for a quick and painless death for one that I loved.

When I returned to her she spoke of how each time she closed her eyes she would see the chaos and feel the evil energy which undulated like the prairie cyclones she remembered from her childhood. Her ears rang with contradicting sounds, the harsh thud of a slab of meat lugged heavily onto the table for her quick knife to carve into smaller pieces was really her husband's body taking blows from fists and sharp-toed boots. She was confused how some of the men could giggle at their fellow comrades lifting her skirt high over her waist. Not the mirthful sound coming from behind small hands clasped over lips, but it was grown men, adults, the type of person who would be shunned in her society, but the white man was more accepting of their own. It physically sickened her to think of the pain her husband must have felt before he did not anymore.

Sometimes one has to see death to know what life is. But the way Never Tamed experienced death throughout her life made her understand all the bad qualities of humans who continued living.

I did not want to be the one who had to do this. I did not want to be the one who allowed a bullet to meet her alive and leave her dead. I could not bear the thought of scratching the surface of her skin, much less forever making the path to her heart indiscernible. In our culture we do not believe in desecrating the body like this, because we believe the spirit needs its body in the afterlife. I begged mercy knowing she would become a spirit we would not talk of, lest we invite her back to haunt us.

And as if I had been spared the duty, I do not remember squeezing my hand around the gun, I do not remember hearing the explosion of the gun, I do not remember feeling the powder burn my hand. And she had spared me too, she had clenched her eyes shut tight and they stayed that way until she was returned back to the earth.

The scent of her fresh blood made me nauseous until my insides made me double over in pain and retch at nothing but the disgust of what the white man would have done to her, knowing that they had no qualms about disrespecting her body while it was still alive and I was reaffirmed that this was the right thing to do. I wiped my mouth clean on my sleeve and looked up to see the trees above my head extended their branches like bent elbows, mocking me, that they were plenty and I could have tied her up high, making any one of them a burial tree.

I set my hands on the hot coals, wanting to feel pain for what I had done, wanting to feel the pain that I had saved her from and the pain I was protecting the boys from also. My heart was selfish when it begged for forgiveness for what my hands had done.

I brought her body to the white law, knowing they would be coming to look for her. At least with her body, they would perhaps forget about the boys until they were far away.

"How did she die? Did you do it?" The man in the uniform asked me, his hand resting on his sidearm.

"Does it matter if it was by her hands, my hands or yours?"

"Did she kill herself?"

"It doesn't matter. She killed a man. She has been punished. She is dead."

"But there are some that would have liked to see her come to justice. We have laws, we have courts."

"We see justice as taking care of our own," I knowingly said, duplicitous in my meaning.

"You have seen her. Now I ask for you to let us bury her."

He didn't answer right away. He had that completive look on his face, probably weighing if letting me take her to bury was a good idea. The pale faces used their Christianity to justify any of their dastardliness, whether it was killing people to save the Christian religion or killing people to convert them to the Christian religion. It would be up to me to give him a choice that didn't necessarily put him in a position that made him look bad, but put us with potentially the upper hand.

81

"With her body we can make her an example of her own crime. Without her body, she will become another martyr." I said quietly, as if I was sharing a secret with him, one that I shouldn't be, more importantly.

I had to lower myself to him. I had to manipulate his sensibilities and cut my own short. We lived in a world ruled by the pale faces and they had shown time and time again, it wasn't a man's character that gained him power or respect, but the color of his skin.

When Momma Got Lost

When Poppa died, everyone was sad. From the far reaches of the county, retired farmers came dressed in their Sunday best and stood around as if they happened to be at the feed store all at the same time. They itched and sweated underneath the starchy shirts and ties with a variety of sport jackets and suits. No one showed up in overalls, even though they all probably wanted to.

Royal Lindale showed up with a cane in one hand and a green tank of oxygen on wheels in the other. Old and shriveled, his skin looked about as alive as the rubber tubing that hung from his ears like a spaghetti noodle passed under his nose.

"Come to offer my condolences," he said to Grandmother as airy as the hiss from the oxygen flowed into his nostrils.

"Thank you," was all she offered to his extended hand. He fumbled to take back the cane from his other hand he had doubled up with devices to keep him moving in the world.

"Some secrets can be taken to the grave," he chuckled as he glanced over at Poppa's casket. "Depends on who's going to the grave."

"Oh, Mr. Lindale," Grandmother practically shouted, as Anna watched her give him one of her steely eyed looks. "Those flowers. Those peonies. I loved them. Thank you for sending them."

Anna did not recall seeing any peonies nor any arrangements sent from Mr. Lindale. He nervously scanned the room as heads turned to look at him.

"Uh, welcome," he flustered and shuffled out the door as quickly as he could.

"Like to light a match and stick it up his ass," Momma said none too quiet.

"You want me to do something, Momma?" Nick asked playfully. Uncle Wes just chuckled. Grandmother seemed to be over it and was being swallowed up in a pink hug coming from Mrs. O'Henry.

But it was after Grandmother died, after the services, the tears, the casket buried in the earth, did things feel like they fell apart. At least for Momma it did. For Anna, everything began to make sense.

Momma hated going to the farm alone. Uncle Wes had come a few times to move furniture around or out of the house. He did not have the patience for diddling with the kitchen stuff or knick-knacks. Nick helped a few times until his number had come up shortly after the funeral and was shipped off to boot camp for a tour of Vietnam.

Anna got the job of helping Momma out with the diddily stuff. It was eventually decided that Grandmother's clothes needed going through. Starting with the top drawer, Momma grabbed out bras and underwear and socks and tossed them on the bed. In the back of the drawer was a bible. Momma flipped through it as Anna gathered up the stuff on the bed and put it in a box.

Out of the corner of her eye, she saw a paper fall out and Momma bent over to pick it up. Anna was not too interested in the paper, but more concerned on getting done early enough to take a bath before going out with Jimmy that night.

Anna looked up when Momma cried out and slumped to the bed.

"What's wrong with you?" Anna ran to her side and noticed the yellowed paper wadded up in her hand, while her other hand covered her eyes.

"Your Grandmother," she swallowed hard and grabbed at Anna's arm, "Wasn't my mother."

"What are you talking about?" Anna tried to shake her arm free of Momma's grip. She was talking like she had no sense.

"My mother died," she whispered.

Anna figured going through Grandmother's stuff had shocked her mother into lunacy. A sigh of impatience slipped out of Anna as Momma shoved her fist, with a wad of paper in it, towards her. Anna sat down next to her, hoping that action would pass for sympathy or comfort and spread the paper out on her lap.

It could have been a crazy joke, but Grandmother had no sense of humor. In her distinct handwriting, heavily slanted for speed, she had written out Poppa's words. Anna imagined them sitting at the worn Formica covered kitchen table and Poppa talking slow so Grandmother could keep up as she dictated his words. He had been too afraid to tell Momma while she was alive. Grandmother was too afraid to tell Momma while she was alive.

"She still was my Grandmother," Anna fought to say behind tears. She could not read anymore and handed it back to Momma. "How come they were afraid to tell?" Anna squeaked, wanting to wrap her arms around her mother, but maybe so she could feel her arms around her.

"My mother was Indian. Poppa was an Indian," she uttered, but there was doubt in her voice, like she did not believe.

"We're all Indians," Anna stated like one knows the sun never rises from the west. Heaven only knows the look that crossed her face.

"You knew?" she hissed at Anna.

"Yes," she said, indignantly. "Didn't you?"

Anna did not see her mother's hand rise up to slap her face. "How could you keep this from me? Who told you?"

"Poppa did." The pain burned, but Anna heard his voice say, *"seven generations"* and she saw a little baby crying for its dead mother and Anna knew that little baby was her mother.

"My own daughter," she cried.

"I'm sorry, Momma. It's okay."

"No it's not. I don't even know who I am."

Momma wept all the way home, crumpled up on the passenger side. Anna called Jimmy and said she could not go out, something came up. Momma locked herself in her bedroom and howled for hours. Anna knocked on the door and asked her if she could get her something to eat. Momma would not answer.

Anna sat at the wobbly card table and un-crumpled the letter again and read it in full. She knew nothing of the details of the letter, just Poppa's secret with her. All this time Anna thought it was the family's secret they all shared, but it had really been only her and Poppa.

Anna had to get the bitter taste of Momma's sorrow out of her head, but her mother was not talking and no one else would do to talk with, since they would not be family. Uncle Wes was out of the question at that moment. Anna really did not want to deal with him breaking down. It was selfish of her, but he would know soon enough. Apparently Grandmother and Poppa had kept the secret from him too.

After several hours of being alone with her thoughts and want for something constructive to do, Anna found some paper and started a letter to Nick. She considered this might be bad news for him, but then again, his last letter described pretty dismal conditions. It would not be fair to leave him out of the family going-ons.

Anna told him how Grandmother had safe-guarded that letter for years, not in the Bible, per se, but in with her undergarments where no one would dare put their prints on something she put against those private spots of her bare skin.

She told Nick what Grandmother had written describing how when Momma was a baby and when her mother died, Grandmother had come to Poppa's rescue. Uncle Wes was born after they were married. Grandmother had raised Momma like her own and hid the facts of her real mother. To protect Momma. To protect Poppa.

As a widower, Poppa was afraid of losing his precious daughter to the Indian schools. He, himself, had suffered his own government-sponsored Catholic abduction from his family. Grandmother knew the only way to safeguard her was to shed all Indian ways. But he could not make his heart comply, regardless of his own time at the Indian school and people's bad opinion of Indians.

Anna had learned to be quiet about the sentiments others had about Indians being lazy, alcoholic and dumb. She knew Poppa was a smart man and hard working, which is why people respected him. It was important to him that his children knew and all their children knew who they were. As much as Poppa tried to make Grandmother bend to his wishes, she would only agree to it after both of them were dead.

After Grandmother died, Momma went into an angry depression. She lashed out at Poppa and Grandmother, even though they were both dead. She was mad at them, as she saw it, for lying to her.

"I watched her belly grow with Wes. I imagined I had spent time there too," Momma sat at the table with her hands in her lap. She stared at them with defeat.

"Are you mad at her? Your real momma?" Anna asked, real sincerity this time.

"No. I'm mad at Poppa, how could he do that to me if he really loved me?" She touched her lips, as if she was surprised at what she said. "It was so unfair for him to not let me know."

When Anna asked if it would have changed anything, Momma got red in the face and shook with clenched teeth. "If I had known I was an Indian, I would have hid it and guarded it with my life. How embarrassing, unlike you who kept the secret to have as your own little treasure, like you get at the fair or a Cracker Jack box. Junk. That's what it is. Worthless. He didn't have to hide it from me. What makes you so special, Anna?"

"Why do you think he hid it from you?" Anna fought back, feeling it was unfair to be blamed for something she had nothing to do with. "From the rest of the world?"

Momma slapped Anna's face. "I never thought my own daughter would betray me."

Sometimes it was just Momma's words that would sting Anna and she would cry silently, only letting the tears run down her face when she felt her relationship with Poppa being attacked.

"You always blubbering about something," Momma would say disgusted. Anna learned to hold those tears in, pretending to be strong, learning discipline, when all she was really doing was holding back tears until they collected and became a flood. She tried to hold back, hoping to save herself and even Momma for that matter and something had to give. A weak spot always developed with that much force weighing against it constantly.

It did not take long before Momma became suspicious of Anna's relationship with Nick. "What secrets of his are you keeping from me?" With those suspicious looks, she would comment, "don't know why Poppa liked you best enough to only tell you." It made Anna feel little and defective. When Momma appraised her like this, Poppa's love and affection had become cheapened, making it small and worthless too.

Poppa had lived dangerously by allowing Anna to know who they were and teach her what he could. But he must have trusted her. She did not believe he loved her more than Momma or Uncle Wes or Nick. He had just trusted her.

Time Comes

It feels like the word cancer is everywhere and people are scared to death of it. Don't go out in the sun, don't smoke. Do eat healthy foods, do get health screens. There are marathons, walks, donation drives to raise money to find a cure. There is chemotherapy, surgery, and quack medicine that promise remission. There are support groups to help people cope and pink ribbons to warm one's heart. It's everywhere, yet I find it a shock that I should have it.

More surprising, living in a so called civilized country, the cancer victims who find themselves without the ability to pay are blamed for not taking care of themselves or working hard enough to make sure they can afford such a luxury as health care. This sounds political, but the real irony is a person's health has become a commodity to be bought and sold, rather than a right. So I am more than a victim of cancer and the thought of being a cancer survivor I cannot even consider right now.

Until I received the diagnosis, I wanted to believe that I was my own person. It was denial that the labels given to me in the past no longer hemmed me in, corralled my exploration. Even the labels I liked, such as granddaughter, precious, hope and future. And then there were the labels I did not care for at the time but now greatly miss, such as sister, shadow, tag-a-long. My brother being taken away was like the shelter of a tree cut down, and I was left in the hot sun, and no one to claim for company. The label of daughter was honor turned to regret and disappointment. Being a wife was not what I had envisioned, but the blame really needs to be on who my husband was. Being a single parent and a mother was damn hard work and there was only exhaustion and frustration, no awards handed out. Now I've become a person with cancer.

There was a time when I took all the labels I was and thought I was recreating them. I started with darkening my eyes with liner and shadow and mascara. Bringing the color of a brisk walk to my face with blush and lipstick, trying to cover up my embarrassment of being such a nothing, a negative. My hair, the delicate of strawberries was covered by the rich tones of walnut, signifying strength and respect.

Image is important, so my finger nails were painted fire engine red, the bold color that says I'm confident and can rely on mature femininity and not the softness and delicateness of pink. Even my toenails were manicured to make a statement regardless that they remain concealed under panty hose and pointy shoes all day.

When I was done, I was unable to recognize who I was and had transformed into someone I wanted to be. Someone that I thought my mother could not possibly find fault with. And I could only stay that way if I didn't let anyone to close to me. I can spend eight hours a day with people and when they see me, they see a polished, successful, confident and independent woman. I had confidence behind the makeup and clothes. They hid the lack of confidence I had in myself and what Jimmy and Momma had taken from me too.

Then there was the part that I kept hidden to everyone except for my own daughter, because I wanted her to learn it once, the easy way, that hard work was hard, and the more mistakes she made with her life, the harder the work would be. At night, after I had worked all day and made dinner, I would take the kids with me to work at the factory on the other side of town. On my hands and knees, I would sift through the floor sweepings, picking out the good scraps of cardboard from the dirt. The recycling couldn't have dirt and the recycling couldn't be thrown away, because it was too valuable. So on my hands and knees, at five dollars an hour, I sorted through it, because five dollars an hour bought food and diapers. Cleaning between factory shifts was honest work. Someone had to do it. I had to do it. We needed the money.

Heaven was the coolness of the offices that had been air conditioned all day. Here the workers went to college, got to spend the day sipping hot coffee while they did their work. I went to college too, but lusted after the wrong boy.

I felt sympathy for the factory workers who worked under the bright lights and I imagined, brushed the sweat off their foreheads in the cross breezes made from fans that moved more dust than air. Their only air conditioning came from lingering in front of the refrigerator at lunch break. But those workers even scoffed at the lowest worker and threw their used paper towels to dry their hands on the floor, urinating carelessly in the stalls and at the urinals. I laughed with pity for their wives as I scrubbed the toilets and the soiled floor surrounding it. They would leave half-eaten baloney and cheese on dead white bread on the cafeteria tables along with apple cores and empty pop cans and candy bar wrappers.

After a break from a friend who helped me get a job and the furniture store, I was thankful the five dollars an hour was no longer our financial lifeblood. It was no longer dollars earmarked for food and hopefully could become five dollars an hour for college savings. My daughter complained that she didn't like having to do that kind of work. The cleaning chemicals dried her hands out and the heavy dust made her feel dirty. I had to hold my teenage daughter's face close to mine. I wanted her to realize that her mother was once pretty. My chapped and ruddy hands were once soft with long delicate nails.

"Beauty isn't everything," I told her. "You need to take your school seriously." My daughter's eyes laughed at me despite the pout her mouth made. She *doesn't understand*, I thought. *She doesn't understand*, I'm sure my daughter thought.

"The money I make at washing toilets is for your college. If you don't want to go to college, tell me now, so I don't have to keep doing it."

The time came where my daughter used the college money. It became money for food and diapers, again.

"Why sacrifice for something your daughter doesn't want?" I remember her asking me.

"Because that is what love is."

I know my daughter doubted it, she only knew love between her and her boyfriend.

"The time will come when you understand," I told her.

It killed me to watch my daughter take my grandson with her, like I used to. When she was little she would doze in her car seat as the cleaning fumes counteracted the human scent of hard work. When she was older, she would cling to my pant leg, fearful from the noises of the building settling in for the night. Older yet, she helped wipe the windows clean, in hopes that she would learn that this was not the job she wanted to do to support her own babies someday. My daughter now understands what I meant and it is too late, because it was a lesson she had to learn herself.

I felt an apprehension, excitement, knowing that I might leave Theresa's home a different person in her eyes, by telling her things that she didn't know as truths, but perhaps only as rumors at best. She was someone I considered a friend, yet it has been so important for me to uphold a certain image of myself to her for all these years.

Despite that, I struggle with how I was going to tell her, I couldn't just blurt it out. I did not want to be like other people who drop such news with no warning and I'm left there with blankness in my mind and in my mouth, because I don't know what to say. I was bracing myself, knowing if I said it, I would get that look where the person backs away, not wanting to be involved, trying to escape in a cover of invisibility, or maybe believing a new dimension would take over and she could slip through the tear in the dimension of reality fabric. It almost feels easier to keep it to myself, because if I tell one person, will it become so easy that I will tell everyone?

Theresa is the kind of person that can go months without seeing someone but pick up the conversation like she last saw you yesterday. I was apprehensive in telling her about the diagnosis, not sure what I wanted from her, but yet I wanted to share it with someone. I had yet to tell my daughter or son. There was no sense in telling them before I had made a decision on what to do. Theresa saw through that too.

"What do you mean you haven't told them?" she gave me her signature tone used to express incredulous of someone else's stupidity.

"I don't want to tell them until I've decided what I'm going to do."

"It doesn't matter what you are going to do. You just can't hide it from them like that. What makes you think they aren't affected by this too? Don't wait because you think you're protecting them. Don't take it all alone. I know you, Anna. For once, quit trying to be a super woman."

She was not easily duped by my charades all these years. I appreciated how she balanced our friendship while flushing me out of my own fantasies as needed. But this time, she hadn't considered the things that were out of my control.

"I know the obstacles. I don't have health insurance and I don't have that kind of money to pay for treatment. Health insurance isn't a spaghetti dinner. I don't begrudge the people who do those fundraisers, it's just a terrible way to rely on getting cured."

"You're right, but they deserve to know. You can't hide a secret like that from them. They're your kids. You're all the family they know."

There was something in what she said that hurt so much. She had found that vulnerable spot without knowing it. Momma had accused me of hiding the secret of who she was all those years. I did it because I didn't want to hurt her. I had done it for Poppa, because he asked me to. I could not talk myself into getting a grip and I felt my face go hot and the tears run out of my face. I wiped at them irritated because I had no control over my emotions. I had no control over my body. I felt her hand touch mine and I wanted to pull away, but she started talking all soft, the brass gone from her usual conversation.

"Didn't your grandfather die of cancer?"

"Yes, he did."

"Is there a history of it in your family?"

"My mother didn't seem to have any of those problems. Nick was killed before he could get old enough."

"How about your grandmother?"

"She wasn't blood to my mother."

"I never knew that."

"Well, we never knew it until she died. Only then did we find out the secret that she had married Poppa after my mother's real mother died."

"Why on earth did they keep that a secret?"

"They were Indians," I hesitated as I felt the muscles in my neck stiffen. "Ojibwe. They kept that secret too because they didn't want the government taking my mother to one of the boarding schools." I said it fast, like it didn't matter, hoping she would not hear or understand what I was saying and what it really meant.

"I didn't know you were Indian. Native American," she added, saying thoughts that finally caught up to her mouth. "Usually I don't tell people about this woman I go to, but when I had all that fibromyalgia stuff going on, and some people were saying I was making it up, I went to this holistic doctor, not really a doctor like in the sense we know of, but a medicine woman. She was able to help me deal with the pain I was feeling. If it was in my head, I don't care, it helped me. It decreased the pain. I don't know if you'd be interested in her, but heck, give it a try if nothing else."

With my secrets brought to life with Theresa, I felt stronger and less vulnerable as keeping them as my own. Yet I had not made attempts to teach what I knew to my children or grandchildren. I now understood what she meant that it was unfair of me to keep the diagnosis from them.

Hierarchy

Royal Lindale stopped his fancy new Lincoln Continental in the driveway. His window was down and his ruddy face could be seen gawking at his destination. Uncle Wes had been rambling at Poppa the other day how he saw how Royal Lindale was playing show-and-tell near the four corners of town, people honking as they passed him holding the suicide doors open to let his grandchildren out. Anna had been bold enough to ask what suicide doors were.

"They open like this," Nick snorted, like everyone knew what they were and showed her, flinging his arms out, hinged at the elbows.

"Oh, like the doors at church," Anna relayed her understanding. This made Poppa and Uncle Wes laugh.

Anna did not know what was so fancy about this car. It was so square, she was not sure if he was driving it backwards or not. The black paint was dusty from the dirt road and most likely hot to the touch as the sun beat down, sending blinding wayward rays off of the chrome.

Heinz jumped up from his usual station on the

front yard and started barked at the man. The usual wagging tail was between his hind legs and the fur on his scruff was puffed out. Mr. Lindale ignored Anna and her little cousin, Tammy, who were playing out in the yard until he realized the dog was not going to let him take a step.

"Call your dog," he demanded.

Nick came around the side of the house and ran to grab Heinz, so to allow Mr. Lindale to leave his car. The girls stared at Mr. Lindale as he approached the front porch of the house. His light blue seersucker dress pants made Anna think he was wearing pajama bottoms with suspenders and a white dress shirt. Everyone else always used the back door to the kitchen, but Mr. Lindale, being a proper gentleman knew to use the front entrance. He stopped short of the steps and turned to look at Grandmother's rose-peony. Poppa had come around the side of the house.

"Mr. Lindale," Poppa greeted cheerfully.

"You got something mighty fine here," Mr. Lindale pointed at one of the clustered blooms on the rose-peony. "Bet you don't' even know what it is," he sneered, eyeing Poppa.

"Actually, I do."

"You know corn," Mr. Lindale said, caressing the bloom in his palm, cupping his hand to the shape of the fragrant petals. "You don't know what you got. I know what you've got."

Poppa shoved his balled up fists in his coverall pockets. Grandmother showed herself at the front door, keeping the screen door latched between them. "I'd invite you in for something to drink, but I haven't anything made."

100

Mr. Lindale chuckled. "You don't worry about me. If I need something, I'll take care of it."

It wasn't until Momma was driving home that evening did Anna understand who Mr. Lindale was.

Momma asked, "What did you do today, Anna?"

"Helped Grandmother a while."

"Yeah?"

"Mr. Lindale came to the house."

"Mr. Lindale? She didn't mention that." Anna watched her mother's head snap in her direction.

"Granny let me have it 'cause Heinz was barking and frothing at him," Nick added.

"What?" Momma asked, sounding sidetracked.

"Heinz hadn't even bit the bastard and was actin' rabid."

"Nicholas Martin, you watch your mouth."

"That's what Granny called him."

"Oh, I doubt that."

"She did," Anna confirmed. "But it was under her breath after he left."

"That I don't doubt."

"How come Grandmother and Poppa don't like him?" Anna asked.

"It's a long story," a crease formed on Momma's usually smooth forehead. "You kids don't go tellin' everyone in the county you know."

"Your secret's safe with me, little lady," Nick said from the backseat and wrapped a sweaty arm around Momma's shoulders.

"I'm serious, boy. Sit down."

"I'm listening," Anna tried to act grown up and serious.

Momma sighed heavy and started telling them what she knew. "When Poppa bought the farm, he bought the land from William Dunlap. Poppa had done favor after favor for him. He agreed to pay Mr. Dunlap a fair price in agreement not to advertise the sale. Mr. Lindale was buying up every bit of property, miles deep on either side of the highway, speculating on something, but never let anyone in on what it was. Mr. Lindale was mad for two reasons, he wanted Dunlap's farm and Poppa did not need to sharecrop for him anymore."

"As punishment, Mr. Lindale required Poppa to work Rock Farm, over on Greer Road. You know how your Grandmother constantly gripes about Poppa killing himself trying to farm that field of rocks and boulders."

"How could he require Poppa to farm it?" Nick had wanted to know.

"Don't know, baby. Don't know why Poppa would do that," Momma glanced back at Nick in the back seat of the car. "Trying to do a favor, knowing your Poppa. Can't believe your Grandmother stands for it."

Anna liked visiting Rock Farm with Poppa. If she stayed quiet enough, he would temporarily forgot she was there and she could watch his face transform into something old, something from the past carved into the crevices surrounding his eyes that had seen things and etched deep around his mouth that had said things, back when the country was wild. She kept quiet and did not question Poppa, afraid he would decide not to bring her next time. It was like his tears that dampened her forehead when she rode on his lap so close and safe, the noise of the tractor was the only thing that distanced them from each other.

She was convinced she understood how those tears meant something like the look on his face, signifying a pitiful sorrow and a want so painful. When the other girls in school would be having so much fun, Anna knew she could not play with them because they made fun of her mother being divorced and laughed at her homemade dresses.

It was unsettling to think Rock Farm might have a different meaning to the family, when Anna cherished her time spent there and yet it caused Poppa so much pain. She rode the rest of the way home without talking, only trying to sort out the jumble in her head. The scenery passed along, framed by the open window, but she only sawn Poppa in her mind.

That Sunday, after church, Poppa pulled into the yard. Anna and her brother jumped down from the bed of the truck. Everyone headed to the back door in anticipation of nourishment for their bodies after an hour of mind-numbing nourishment for their souls, except for Grandmother who started for the front door.

"Where are you going, Grandmother?" Anna asked.

Grandmother did not respond, her determined stride got Poppa and Nick's attention, and they followed. Grandmother stopped at the front porch and stared at the hole as mounds of dirt spilled onto the grass.

"I'll kill the bastard," Poppa swore, something Anna rarely heard from him. Grandmother turned her head and looked at him.

"Where's Heinz?" Nick asked, looking around the yard. "Heinz, Heinz," he yelled with his hands cupped around his mouth. Poppa scanned the yard and into the fields around the house.

"Catherine, take the children into the house," he commanded Grandmother and escorted them in the back door. Anna felt a chill of a wind go through her in the otherwise oppressive swelter from the heat of the day. He went back out with his hunting rifle as Grandmother was getting lunch started. Anna helped set the table all the while waiting to hear the sound of the gun. There was a stiffness in the air that Poppa had left. She wished she could have asked him why he took the gun, but the apprehension had rendered her mouth dry of words, Grandmother's too, when she thought about it, as no one spoke. Poppa came back after a while with dirt on his boots from scraping the dirt back into the hole where the peony had been. Without explanation, he put the gun away and sat down to lunch.

Scissors

Big Brother felt the smooth chill from the scissors as he ran his fingers gently across the sharp beaks. He held them in the waist of his pants, inside, against his skin, waiting until the boys were allowed outside and he could bury them. He knew that if he hid them inside the buildings, they would be found. It would be discovered soon enough that they had disappeared. Feeling the coolness of the metal, he knew the beaks of the scissors held power. With them, they gave the holder the power to cut another's spirit. They could be used for evilness, but Big Brother wanted them and was sure that he could use them for good, if nothing else they could not be used to hurt any more of the boys. The cold season was coming and he would have time to plan how he would use them to take Little Brother back to his parents.

Out under the vast blue sky, the wind whispered in a different voice across the vast fields, compared to the protective shush-shushes of the trees of the forest back home. Big Brother imagined the sound of the flute, teasing like the wind, the way it mimicked the cooing sounds of birds and the howl of wolves. The wail of the wind with no one to talk back to, except the grasses that could only mustered a weak whisper back. It sounded sad sometimes, as if it knew all that had happened, it remembered all the chiefs and braves, the mothers and fathers and all of their children. It spoke of the bravery it had seen and wanted to warn of what was yet to come.

"Thomas," Sister Therese yelled at him. "Come back with the rest of the group." He had wandered again too far at the edges of the school perimeter.

Father Xavier told the children they must stay on the school property, the land that the church owns. The first time they were told this, a little boy, who still had not accepted he no longer lived in the native world, said "You do not own the land, it is Mother Earth's." That had earned him a whipping and all of those who dared to stand up for what they knew as true.

The boys and girls were kept in separate buildings and only saw each other at meal times and worship. But they were still segregated on either side of the rooms. Both of these times they were to be silent. They were also required to be silent, except when called on, while at school. It was hard to sit at the tables and chairs for lessons. If they had been taught anything while living in the wilderness, it was respect for elders, which gave them the patience to endure the Sisters abrading reprimands.

The big boys were regularly hit and slapped and whipped. Father Xavier had been heard telling the Sisters the big boys had to be torn down and rebuilt. Their savage ways had to literally be beaten out of them to make room for decent civilized society and Christianity. The little boys were beat, being told there was hope for their wretched souls, being young enough that they were still malleable, like soft clay. The boys were forced to communicate in English and they quickly learned what 'stupid,' and 'ignorant' meant, as these people who professed to be servants of their lord, used these words often. It was understandable to Big Brother that they might feel oppressed by the thankless responsibility they were given and felt they had to take it out on the Indian boys and girls under their care. He could feel his own anger, like fine grains of sand, eroding his discipline to obey Father Xavier and the Sisters.

But the nasty names the children were called were not as severe as being told they would no longer be allowed to call themselves by their names, but would have to now go by names Father Xavier had picked out for them. The names were harsh to their ears, they felt unimportant as they did not describe anything about the individual. That was the start of when fear left many of their eyes, and the look of desperation, of being lost became their new awareness. Even Big Brother learned to obey whatever command was asked of him when called by the new name of Thomas he had been given by Father Xavier.

They were taught the different names of the Great Fathers in a place called Washington. George Washington, Thomas Jefferson, Abraham Lincoln, General Grant and Teddy Roosevelt. The Great Father's name at the moment was Woodrow Wilson. The entire world seemed to be at war with each other. The German tribe of pale faces had started the trouble and a king, who they called Tzar, had been killed in a land called Russia. His whole family had been slaughtered. Was this war worse than the Civil War or the Revolutionary

War, one child timidly asked. Another child got caught up in the discussion and said he remembered hearing stories of his grandfather fighting the pale faces.

"What war would that have been, Sister Therese?" he asked.

"Those were the Indian Wars, and the United States finally won. The battle at Wounded Knee Creek punished the Indians for their horrible slaughter of General Custer and his men," Sister Therese was caught up in the discussion too, as her voice ended in an high pitched fever.

With that, Big Brother understood why they were told to forget their rituals because they were pagan and savage and they needed to become civilized. He understood why they were told not to speak their language because it was forbidden. They were being punished for what they would not give the white man and the white man did not want to give anything back in return. At least when gifts are given, it is because one respects the receiver. The Indians could not give the land to the white man, as it was not theirs to give.

The boys were lined up for the special meeting that the sisters said Father Xavier had asked for. Father Xavier had something important to discuss. Big Brother felt dread. He knew if Father Xavier was involved, someone would end up getting whipped with the black snake. The boys whispered rumors of what might have happened and who might be in trouble when the sister's backs were turned.

Father Xavier standing tall in his black robes, looking darker with the sunlit window behind him and his face disappearing into the shadows, spoke in a tone that vibrated into each boys chest until they all breathed out fear. The scissors were missing and Father Xavier also told them God knew who had taken them and there was no way to hide from God's all knowing eyes. The boys squirmed as they stood at attention, knowing Father Xavier would never believe the scissors were lost. They had been told over and over that they were thieves with no guilty conscience and would steal anything. Food, they stole all the time, but to the boys it was less about stealing and more about their empty bellies. Father Xavier told the boys that God would forgive the boy who confessed to knowing who did it, so the sinner could be punished. Not one boy raised his hand. The boys looked at the dusty tops of the shoes of Brother Michael and the sisters walking back and forth in front of them that clomped heavily, refusing to make eye contact with anyone.

"Who is the guilty one? Confess and let Jesus cleanse your heart," Father Xavier thundered. He turned on his heel and grabbed one of the little boys up by the arm. "Tell me what you know."

"Does the person who took the scissors get a whipping because Jesus cleans their heart?" The boy said in a pleading voice.

With that Father Xavier dragged the boy over to a chair and sat down, forcing the boy down across his lap and started spanking him with his bare hands.

"By God, you bastard heathens will know the pain of being a sinner," he yelled with hot breath.

All the boys got whipped. One by one, Father Xavier gave them their punishment and did not enlist Brother Michael or the Sisters to relieve his weary arms other than to guide the next boy to him. The sobbing and the crying of the little ones with no one to comfort them was a sound they were getting use to hearing. Being raised with the earth and the sky as parents and protectors and providers, the Indian boys and girls found their world inhospitable, but more importantly, they realized another human could make the world so un-welcoming with their convictions of righteousness.

The little boys would cry and cry each night for their mothers. Their fathers. Eventually they quit crying. Big Brother figured their memories of home had faded and they could not cry over things they could not remember. The sparkle of wonder in the young boys eyes were replaced with glassy stares and their mouths set in stone. The only smiles to be seen were Sister Angeline's and Brother Michael's.

Sister Angeline would sometimes come into the dormitory at night and pick up an inconsolable boy out of his bed and rock him back and forth and sing to him. Her soft voice soothed the ears, drowning out the harshness of the voices from the day. She would slip back out, her shoulders and head showing her tiredness.

Big Brother figured it was his own spirit Father Xavier and Brother Michael, with their hungry eyes, wanted. If anyone was going to have his spirit, Big Brother would have to save his own, so he determined to close his ears against the crazy, odd logic the pale faces used to explain their 'religion.' Father Xavier and Brother Michael and the Sisters seemed to travel a path that led only one way. With each step forward, they demanded that the boys show them respect, yet in their wake, they threw their garbage on the face of Mother Earth and stabbed at her heart with metal spades to turn the dirt over.

It was like a cloudy night, when the sky was empty of stars; the spirits of the children were slowly becoming invisible. The spirits that had not died, had fled, run away, leaving only empty shells. Big Brother hid his spirit and was determined to take it back to mother and father. Take Little Brother too, even if it was only the shell. At least they would know it was their son who haunted them.

White Man Blackmail

It had only taken twenty-some odd years for life to become something Catherine wanted. She had been so naïve, even if she was old enough to be considered a spinster, back then, before repeating her wedding vows. Even though there had never been regret for trading in the dusty chalk squeaking across the ashy slate to wrap her fingers around all the tasks on the farm to make the family's life go from day to day, she had expected that there would be more that she could call her own after years of diligent hard work.

She and her sister had been poor after their parents had died, but Catherine learned of a different kind of poor when it was babies wailing, competing with their own grumbling stomachs. She knew how to cook and clean and which end of a book to hold up, but things like cultivating a garden or animal husbandry she depended on Thomas to teach her. He knew how to do everything. Nevertheless, it was she, who learned what she could, knowing enough to winnow out the Indian teachings and not to draw attention to the family where even the little ones did not know the secrets. They would never know the secrets if it was up to Catherine. Slowly, she accepted how the dirt stained the cracks in her hands and learned to appreciate the animal smells, which equated to their survival.

She learned to make something from nothing, by mixing the ash water with rendered fat to make soap in a cast iron cauldron hanging over a bed of warm coals. Stirring and stirring with a big wooden paddle until she wanted to cry from the ache in her arms, her hair windblown and smoky, hanging in her face, sticking to the sweat. She cut short Lillian and Weston's complaints that the other children made fun of their homemade dresses and shirts. There was so much they did not know about what made a person respectable. All the fancy stitched clothes from the store still would not guarantee a person good on the inside of their skin. Being ever practical, she even belittled herself to think her world would ever be anything but backwards and convoluted. She chewed the bitter fibers of discontent until they were mashed unrecognizable before swallowing, forcing them to nourish her maturity.

Thomas had been as hard working and as good of a husband that she could have ever wished for, even changing her mind that all men were selfish and arrogant. Try as he might, he had yet to transform her negative convictions regarding mankind. More importantly, between them they had raised two children, who were surprisingly generous. It humbled Catherine when they forced her and Thomas to accept their hard-earned dollars and buy a farm. It would be more than a place they could call their own. It would be freedom, after all those years of sharecropping for a man who believed stacking the odds in his own favor was fair. He justified taking a little more each year for his risk, his hard work. Apparently, a man could be that smug with clean fingernails and soft palms, not even a callous where he might grip a pen, as he toiled over cultivating his wealth. Catherine was sure the only sweat he might work up would be over a pretty girl who wasn't his wife, whose mouth whispered garish rumors about others in a perpetual churlish grin.

Their children, now adults, were both gainfully employed, married and swimming along with the hard current of their own lives. Lillian's first baby was just weeks away from making its entrance into the world. Thomas was a grinning fool, in anticipation of this baby. Of course he had been excited about Weston's birth, decades ago, and even helpful, but the thought of a grandbaby had him tickled. She was looking forward to the baby's birth too, but excitement was a feature best kept in line with hard work and confined to only a smile.

Catherine wondered if the whole move to the farm was heightened as if everyone was in nesting mode, getting ready for the new baby. Of course, Lillian and her husband had their own tiny apartment in town, but the farm would be home. It would be home as she cleaned the old dirt out and they made their new tracks to each corner of the house. The bare necessities had been unpacked, but with so many other things that needed to be fixed before proceeding, things like the china cabinet were still empty. With a few unassigned moments, Catherine decided it was way past time to unpack the mismatched pieces of good dishes and tablecloths from the cardboard box, which was a little dusty from sitting in the corner so long. Catherine had supervised Lillian packing each platter and bowl with lots of newspaper because sometimes Lillian's mind became distracted from the task at hand. She was glad to see everything had made it in one piece. She was stuffing all the newspaper back into the box when she heard a loud rapping. Catherine made her way to the front door, trying to figure out who would be banging on the front door with such hostile and impatient fervor.

Royal Lindale stood on the edge of the porch with his hands on his hips, looking everything over with a critical eye, not in the least bit trying to hide what he was doing. His straw hat was pushed back on his head, like a frivolous accessory, all that seemed missing was a band of red, white and blue that he could have waved to the crowds lining a parade route. This was her property, she owned it free and clear, nothing to do with him. Ordinarily she took it as a mild irritation when he came to the door, like the foreboding hum of mosquitoes because it was that time of year, but that was when they were renting from him. For him to cast his darkness on her property was another matter. Did he honestly believe he owned them? She was doubtful the lush green fields he owned conjured up feelings of pride or beauty, but instead evoked that dark color of jealousy void of any brightness for the fields he didn't own.

With her husband in town, she felt a bit scared having to deal with Royal Lindale alone. It was just a feeling, but she knew one did not willingly show their weaknesses to the devil.

"You've gone and made a big mistake," he bellowed.

"Excuse me?"

"You'll lose everything trying to make this farm

go. You tell your husband to come see me. I thought he was smarter than this to get himself into something that has failure written all over it."

"It sounds like you already knew he wasn't home. Why didn't you wait until he was here?"

"Ungrateful. That's what you are." He finally took his hat off, not out of respect, but to wave it around in resentment. "I was taking care of you, looking out for you when no one else would rent to you."

Catherine clenched her teeth and counted to three. What they thought an opportunity so many years ago had really been a prison sentence, renting from him with the intent to save for their own farm. He had kept them on such a pittance and regularly changing his promises for lies every time it might let them get ahead. It spited her to think she had to raise two children to adulthood so they could earn enough money to escape Mr. Lindale's indentured clutches, as if she and her husband were deficient.

"This is our chance to get ahead and have something to call our own.'

"You gotta have money to make money and your husband doesn't have the brains to know the difference between fool's gold and money. You make sure you send your husband my way," he said, taking a step down off the porch.

"We've paid your rent in full. You have nothing else coming from us. We've got no business with you anymore."

With that, he tipped his hat and spat on the front porch, purposefully when the front yard was two steps away from him at that point.

Catherine had felt on edge since Royal Lindale's visit. She had told Thomas, making it as if it had not bothered her, but she kept looking out the windows whenever she heard a vehicle coming down the road. It was she, who alerted Thomas that Mr. Lindale had returned. He had just finished lunch and was on the back porch putting on his muddy work boots. Disregarding Catherine's past fussing that his work boots were only allowed on the porch, he tromped through the house with Catherine trailing his wake with pursed lips. She stayed on the inside of the screen door and watched him walk to the edge of the front porch and fold his arms in front of him, not allowing Mr. Lindale to step up.

"If you have any business with me, you come to me," Thomas dared to look the man in the eye. "Don't bother my wife."

Mr. Lindale chided him. "Oh, you don't have to worry about me harassing that old school marm," his chuckle was like rocks being dumped into a pile. "She was getting too old, until you came along. Yep. A man likes his meat rare, full of flavor you know. You strike me as a grizzle man. Likes to do a lot of chawn'. She still was never as purty as your injun wife."

"What do you want from us?" he demanded of Mr. Lindale.

"Look, I'm just trying to look out for you. I got some land on Greer Road that needs to be rented. You can farm that."

"I dunno. That's pretty rocky soil over there. I don't know if it's worth it. I appreciate the offer though."

"I'll make it worth it to you. Nobody around here knows you, if you want to keep it that way, I'll look out for you."

Catherine seethed, angry that this man would use her husband's own truths against him, threatening to render him incapacitated. How he knew, she could only imagine. Confrontation would only confirm to Mr. Lindale that they accepted it as a threat. It hurt her to see her husband humiliated and taken advantage of when he was already too generous to others. She recalled, fleetingly, sometimes in the darkness of their bedroom, Thomas would tell her stories about his childhood, always relating to how he was taught to listen to his feelings and intuition, which she always invalidated as savage. With the screen door separating them, she felt a surge to the tips of her fingers and radiating outward to the rest of her body, a roar of a primal instinct to protect him. She forced her mind to paralyze acting on her urge. He would not hurt anyone, she knew from years of living with him. She had promised so long ago, to keep his secret for his little girl. The promise, which had evolved into a commitment to protect him, now included the whole family.

"No need to tell me now. I'll let you digest this tidbit for now," Mr. Lindale said all smiles and chuckled as he made his way to the car. Sometimes a person might laugh to relieve anxiety, but Catherine knew Mr. Lindale's was for the sheer purpose of making them feel inferior.

From the other side of the screen door she watched Mr. Lindale's car pull out of the drive and take off too fast, kicking up dust behind him. Thomas left the front porch and made his way quietly to the barn without speaking to her. She did not bother to say anything to him either, since there was nothing new they could say about the secrets they kept. She stayed leaning on the doorjamb, believing that the devil must surely be able to take the form of a man, following them, tormenting them from the peace they sought.

All these years she knew the hurt Lillian and Weston complained about receiving from the Lindale children had been real and it squeezed at her heart. Telling them the secrets she knew about those children bred by arrogance would have reprised the taunting Lillian and Weston had endured. Instead, she accused her own children of exaggeration. She could never comfort those two in the face of those playground taunts, because then it would be their own mother admitting that they were inferior.

Becoming Anna

Poppa's death really did not affect Anna in a negative way until Momma denounced him. Anna wanted to plug her ears and yet at her mother, "you don't understand Poppa, he would never hurt you." But that would have confirmed Anna's allegiance and her mother already felt everyone was out to get her. With each cutting remark and put down against Poppa, Anna built her resentment against Momma, brick by brick.

When Momma found out she was Indian, she wanted to distance herself as much from what she called heathen ways. She armed herself with the words from the Bible, all the negative ones it seemed like to Anna. All the ones that allowed her to judge everyone else, she used liberally, as she took her new position seriously, as lieutenant to God himself. Embracing her Christian faith even tighter, she condemned Poppa for his pagan ways.

"Burning in Hell right now. Hope those flames are licking at his un-Christian soul." Momma's rants forced Anna to discount Poppa's teaching of the native ways and thinking, just to keep the rift between them from becoming a bigger chasm of ugliness.

She was able to escape a goodly portion of her time between working and taking classes at the community college. Anna's mother thought college wasn't necessarily the route she should take. She was suspect of those with college learning, like they were raising their noses all the time trying to balance their heads full of brains.

"I spent a lifetime with my nose to the grindstone. An honest person will hold their head humbly, while their shoulders are strong, broad from working. Just don't get too smart. No man will want that." Before being attacked with her mother's stinging words, she used to be proud of her Momma, not needing any man to be a constant in her life for survival. Anna now doubted her mother's tips for keeping a man, as she had never kept one for too long.

The college classes were hard, but they made the world opening up for her. She had never had such exposure to so many new ideas from not just the instructors but her fellow classmates. These new ways of thinking reminded her of how Poppa looked at the world differently than the people they knew. She knew why he did and continued to keep his secrets so not to hurt others, especially Grandmother. Now that both of them were dead, there weren't any secrets, but she still did not feel safe talking about them. Whatever it was, that allowed people to think differently and share their views, she wanted to know, as she desperately sought validation for what she felt.

Friendly with her smile, she wasn't threatening and just about anyone she wanted to talk to would engage. There was a boy who sat in the back of the class where Anna usually sat. He had a soft voice and was always so polite. Not like the other boys were strutting and drawing attention to themselves. Anna figured her new friend, Lincoln, was purposeful in being quiet and unassuming. She had already seen what happened to the black boys who weren't.

The fact that Lincoln was black eventually slipped into Anna's conversation with Momma. Her mother still called them niggers, the word jumping from her lips in disgust, as if it were a piece of bitter pith she was trying to spit out of her mouth.

"Associating with people like that will get you in trouble," Momma snorted and pointed her fork at Anna to make it clear she was speaking to her, even though they were alone in the house. "The bible says we are not to mix."

Poppa never seemed to worry about mixing and working and joking with Bob and Jake who used to come and help him. He treated them like they were equals, just plain human beings. But with Momma's condemnation of Poppa's true heritage, Anna considered Poppa might have been just as equal to Bob and Jake in the eyes of white folk.

"You just stay away from those niggers. You don't want nothin' to do with them."

She was well aware of the civil rights tumult, but this was the nineteen seventies. Integration had happened so it just seemed logical that acceptance would be the next step. She asked for clarification from her mother. "You mean like the dirty, lazy Indians?" she repeated the words she had heard Momma use to define her own flesh before she knew.

She watched her mother's hand raise up to strike her. Anna did not move, daring her mother and then feeling her hand hit her face like a hot branding iron. She felt all of her mother's hot anger sear into her where her hand had made contact with her flesh.

"When you have everything you love taken away from you and then told everything you've ever known is false, then you can judge me," her mother said after retracting her hand from Anna's face.

The words vibrated into Anna's ears, hearing them as noise, refusing to acknowledge them. She only concentrated on letting her own anger, loathing, hatred for her mother to color her cheeks with anger.

Momma had let it slip to Jimmy. It was her way of getting back at Anna for thinking too much for herself and it was the kind of thinking that Momma professed would surely get her into trouble. She had willingly played on Jimmy's vulnerabilities that got him to take ownership of her own daughter in ways that fed his manliness. He took it upon himself to follow Anna to the college and strolled in at the beginning of class and stood next to her.

"Anna," he said calmly.

"What are you doing here?" Anna whirled around in her seat in surprise.

"Seeing how you're learning to like niggers here at college," he said with no shame.

Anna flushed with embarrassment as the instructor glared at Jimmy.

"You are going to have to leave," the instructor pushed. "I need to start the class."

"I think he's a nigger lover too," Jimmy pointed over his shoulder with his thumb towards the instructor. "You gonna sit here and be brainwashed?"

Embarrassment made her insides feel like they were melting and she slid out of her chair and walked past him, embracing her books tight against her chest. Running down the hall, she escaped into the women's restroom. Shame burned hot on her cheeks as she thought how Poppa had pretended to be white, because that was the only way he could be accepted. It did not matter what the facts were, Momma refused to acknowledge that she was anything other than white. Jimmy did not know anything about all of this and was willing to insult Anna in his ignorance. She had to calm down enough to go back to class. Thank goodness it was not the one with Lincoln. Hopefully Jimmy would have lost interest waiting so long and would have gone home when she exited the restroom.

"I'm sorry, Anna," Jimmy stood outside the door and caught her by the arms. "I don't know the right things to say sometimes. I'm not book smart like you are. I'm scared someone is gonna hurt you and I promised Nick that I would take care of you."

Anna could barely keep standing at the mention of Nick. Her heart ached for him and a little selfishly for herself, knowing he would have stood up for her. She doubted Jimmy's confession as Nick never cared for Jimmy. She slid down the wall and did not care that the tears ran down her face furiously. The door of her class swung open and students came out and stared at them as they headed to their next classes. Anna could not avoid the looks she got from a few who dared to make eye contact with her. She had no choice but to let Jimmy lead her out of the building and head back home. Nick was gone and Poppa was gone and maybe

124

Momma was right in all her nastiness that she needed a man to take care of her.

"What's your problem?" Anna heard her mother ask at the dinner table that evening. She did not think Momma deserved an answer with her accusing tone, when it was her, who had stirred up the maliciousness that bubbled beyond her own life. Momma had to know Jimmy would do something so she couldn't go back to school. She couldn't handle the humiliation and now the icy looks from her fellow students as they looked away from her. Momma had succeeded in getting Anna to conform, even if she would not listen to reason.

Anna looked up from her plate and glared at her mother while she answered. "I guess I have a hard time seeing your miserable life getting better when you interfere with mine."

"As long as you live under my roof, you better act like you know right from wrong." Momma, in one fluid movement, grabbed Anna's plate, still full of food, and scraped it into the wastebasket. "All this college learning has done for you, is make you think you're better than all of us."

Anna made the decision that she could not live in her mother's house any longer. But that left her with where to go? It was almost a guilty thought to wish Nick alive and maybe, the fantasy, live with him, even though some might look down on that, a single young girl, but it did not matter, it wasn't going to happen. Sure fire to be scandalous would be to move in with Jimmy, if he didn't live with his parents. He was the lesser of the two evils at the moment and at least in Jimmy's arms she found solace, even if they were kind of rough in handling her. That was just Jimmy.

She played him the next time they went out. "What do you think of getting married?" He was unable to hide how his eyes got big, looking scared, before cloaking himself with the 'I'm tough, whatcha gonna make me do' look.

"It's something I'll probably have to do, one of these days," he said, probably trying to bait her. She gave no response, something he apparently took as a passing whim of hers, not an actual accusation. He leaned over and mashed his lips against her face, tasting her greedily.

"Stop," she said with disgust and pushed him away.

"What's the matter with you?"

"Are we ever gonna get married?" she asked with her arms folded across her chest.

"Aw, babe. I'm too young for that. I don't wanna be pinned down. You heard of a time in a man's life where he needs to sow his wild oats?"

"I don't think you're gonna get to do it rent free on my fields anymore, Jimmy," she said as a vision of Poppa came into her head, big and elbowing its way past all her other thoughts. She forced it back, not wanting to change her mind now about convincing Jimmy into marriage.

Anna was full of determination that she and Jimmy would have a wonderful life and their marriage would be smooth. She was going to be better than Momma, not being divorced and raising two kids by herself. She knew better, ignorant to whether it was arrogance or immaturity.

Marriage for Jimmy was obviously more stressful. Anna's hope of idyllic married life was chipped away when Jimmy would go out with his friends without her. He would tell her when she did not want to stay home, "You're the one who wanted to get married." When she wanted to go out with her friends, he told her no, and when she asked why, he showed her with the palm of his hand. When she told him she was pregnant, his reaction was a little more subdued, lamenting, "shit. I guess my life's over."

She believed her bruises were her own fault. But when the incessant crying of their new baby frustrated them both, Jimmy was less able to handle it and lashed out at Anna before he grabbed the baby and shook her. For everything bad in Anna's life, this baby was everything good, and she could not excuse it anymore as Jimmy struggling to keep his temper in control. She used her own fists, pounding them into his fleshy arms and chest, and explained to him at the top of her lungs that she would kill him if he hurt her baby. It may have been shock that prompted him to beg her forgiveness. But to Jimmy, promises had expiration dates.

When the police came the first time they told her that she needed to be a better wife, to not make him mad after he gave his performance. "I'm so sorry. It will never happen again," he cried with tears for the officers. "I love you, babe. You're my everything. I won't let you walk out that door and you take everything that means anything to me." They let him return to the house to cool down, while Anna refused to go in and stood on the icy sidewalk and shivered.

"I can't live like this," she blubbered with tears streaming down her cheeks until they combined with the snot running down her face. She held the baby in her arms, almost too big to hold for that long. "He's gonna kill me. I can't stay here."

"What are you gonna do? You'll be out on the streets with a baby," the officers tried to reason with her. "You can't do that."

She looked forebodingly at the house and braced her shoulders that felt sore and bruised. Looking back at the house she envisioned what the inside of the house would look like with the color of her blood on the walls. If she stayed, it would happen and she could not shake the feeling, the vision. What it probably meant was her physical death, yet she knew she was already dying on the inside. Between Jimmy and Momma, the only way she could cope was to smother her feelings and emotions.

"If you need help, maybe you should talk to someone at your church, or something."

'Seven generations,' she could hear Poppa whispering to her soul. *'What you see, you can change.'* She looked down at the baby and knew she had to leave for no other reason than for Poppa. It dawned on her how important it was for her to preserve the seven generations for Poppa. That realization also convinced her to leave Jimmy and raise their daughter on her own.

"I'll take care of myself," she said flatly, emotion a vulnerability she couldn't afford anymore.

She convinced Momma to loan her money for a first and last month's rent on an apartment in the city. She would leave the day the divorce papers would be served. No way in hell was she going to stay any longer than that. He would kill her for sure.

Anna got a job on the other side of the city, hoping that Jimmy wouldn't have reason to frequent that side of town. All the time she knew him, he seemed to get what he wanted without going past the twenty mile mark from his house. When she visited Momma she would drive past the college, and look at it wistfully at something that never would be. It did not matter how many trips she made into the big city, she never felt it was hers, just a visitor.

Being a single parent exhausted her to the bones. After a particularly grueling week at work, she picked up her daughter from the babysitter and was heading home, looking forward to falling into bed. Something familiar came into her vision as she turned on to her street, but it was out of context, not in the right place. It was Jimmy's truck in front of the house she rented a room in. She twitched at the feel of all the little hairs on her body standing on end. She drove past it, hoping he was not looking out the windows. She kept driving. There was no way she could face him again. The divorce was not final and in his mind, she knew he felt she was still his wife. She kept driving, remembering that her paycheck had been cashed and was a wad of coins and bills in the bottom of her purse. The baby was getting hungry and probably wet. She kept driving until she was on the highway, going further away from everything she knew. She was wearing her waitress uniform. She did not even go back for the baby toys.

Anna finally knocked on her mother's door late that night. Momma gave her hell for not facing Jimmy. No matter what Anna said, it would not convince her. "You aren't gonna find another man who's gonna take care of you. You just don't know what love is, sure, I believe he's got a temper, but you gotta take responsibility for your part of the marriage."

"No, I'm not going to raise my child like this."

"Just like your grandfather, humiliating the rest of the family."

Anna seethed at her mother's accusation. She wanted to defend this man that was a part of her, even a part of her mother who rejected them both. Then Anna was mad at Poppa for not standing up to Grandmother all those times when she would hush him when he skated the conversation too close to being an Indian. It was his fault that he never was brave enough to say what was right, which in turn, allowed her mother to treat her like this.

And it was the next morning in her mother's house where Jimmy was invited in. "You two need to talk," Momma announced. "I'm going to the store."

Anna was alone with the baby and Jimmy was so pathetic looking and he grabbed her arm crying. "You don't understand Anna, I got to see you. I'm sorry I got mad at you all those times. I haven't stopped loving you." The baby started crying. "See, my own baby doesn't even remember who I am." He let go of her arm. "Please Anna, give me another chance. One last chance." He followed her into the living room where she put the baby into the playpen, hoping to return to the kitchen where their daughter wouldn't have to witness their fighting.

"I gave you all the chances I can give," Anna stated, hoping for composure, as she was sure he could see her shaking as she went back into the kitchen. "I don't trust you. I don't care what my mother says, we have nothing to talk about."

Any safety Anna felt in her mother's house was not enough to protect her from the punch to the face that made her hit the floor just as hard. Stunned, she smelled the alcohol on his breath before she realized he was so close to her because he was on top of her and had her arms pinned to the floor. It did not matter how much she struggled, he pulled her hair and slapped her face when she tried to bite him while he dragged her past the screaming baby and into the bedroom.

She braced herself as he jabbed her hard with the thing he was most proud of, convinced that it proved his manliness. She lay stiff underneath him, every muscle contracted, repulsed by him. "Aw, Anna, that's good and tight, girl. Oh, I've missed this." She started crying and started praying to her mother's God, *'not another baby, not another baby,'* and willed her uterus, her ovaries, her eggs and all that shit to be inhospitable to this intruder. She loved her daughter, even if she was half of this pathetic excuse for a man, but she could not bear the thought of another baby to raise, constantly running away from Jimmy to keep her and the children safe.

The smoke and alcohol seeped through his sweaty pores, creating a heavy and putrid smell that was still stronger and more offensive compared to her own odors. She was use to the smell of her own perspiration; it was a part of her. Except for when it stuck to her uncomfortably with the perfume she wore. He had bought it for her. It was a huge gesture, even though it was a cheap brand from the drug store. She bitterly recalled how she had worn it to show him her appreciation, even though it smelled nothing like it did straight from the bottle after it chemically mixed with her own body chemistry, creating noxious fumes. She lay next to him, trying not to move and stir up more of his scent from the wadded up sheets in the already humid bedroom where the air conditioner blew full blast, barely cooling the room. Soon enough he would be passed out and she could escape him again.

Indigenous Lies

And that is how I sat in front of this woman, this stranger, and spilled my secrets to her, things Poppa had confided in me, promising me to keep secret. The thing Momma was so ashamed of other people knowing about her. There was a tantalizing feeling of disobeying her and finally giving Poppa the respect I didn't think she or Grandmother had given him. Tantalizing, but heart wrenching, by honoring one, I would be dishonoring two. And where did I fit in?

"You're hiding something," the medicine woman said to me, not at all impressed with my ability to stay composed. "You're holding it so tight you won't let go. You're hiding it in your body and your body is tired and weak and isn't able to fight the invaders that entered your body."

"But I'm not hiding anything."

She sat there, staring at me, unashamed of the silence between us. She was waiting me out, daring me to agree with her.

"I have cancer," I said, as if I could accuse her for asking. And I was, feeling awkward as to what she would have to do with it now. I was ashamed for making this woman carry my burden as her own, but I felt relief too, like I couldn't be held responsible for my actions. "I'm sorry."

"That is why you're here," she said more like a statement, not hiding the doubt she had, as if she did not believe me fully.

"I'm tired. My body's exhausted. My mind is exhausted. I don't know if I can continue on. I'm not sure if I want to continue on," I said with rapid fire, wanting her to be sensitive, shaming her into accepting that I was the one who needed understanding. "Cancer is a hard battle. It's even a harder battle, a losing battle, if there is not help from medicine I can't afford. I'm worn out now. Thinking of trying to win this, endure this, makes me even more tired. I don't have the energy to do it. I don't want to do it."

It didn't seem to matter what tactic I took with her, but I was running out of ways to tell her what I needed without telling her things I wasn't sure I needed, wasn't sure I wanted to share, wasn't sure I could share. "I don't want to fight for something I don't feel I deserve."

"Why do you think that?"

And she made me think. I guess I never allowed myself to think there was an answer to that. Could I deserve what I hadn't earned and what I tried so hard to be and never succeeded? Should I feel proud about keeping a secret when I couldn't stand up for what was right?

My thoughts all came to the same conclusion. After Poppa and Grandmother died, everything I felt good about had been taken away. My mother made me feel that everything about me was bad. I no longer had worth in her eyes. It was the ultimate rejection. Like the quivering noise of the bow drawn against the string of a violin which has taken someone years of practice to make it become music, it has taken just as much time and diligence to create in my mind that I was unworthy, incompetent and a thing of ugliness, repulsiveness in her heart.

"My mother hated knowing she was Indian." I felt a dread, an apprehension before telling her, like a kid with a secret, wanting to be the first to tell what they aren't suppose to. I had kept that secret for so long; like Poppa had taught me and Momma ended up hating me for doing it.

"This was your mother's pain and you have made it yours," she sighed with sympathy, a whole new emotion from her that crumbled the harsh walls I felt were between us. "You have to destroy what you have allowed yourself to become with your mother's words. You have to rebuild who you are."

"But who I've been has never been good enough for her. She disliked that I was accepting of being an Indian. I wasn't ashamed until she made me."

"You have no reason to be ashamed of who you are. That means what your roots are too. No one can make you feel ashamed of who you are, except for yourself."

"That's not fair. You are blaming me."

"Come back down to earth, where things really are," she sneered and raised her hands toward the ceiling. "Up there you forget you are the one in control, any pain you feel, you absorb, when you could stop it. Don't get me wrong, pain is good to remember, it makes you careful as you step into the depth of the stream, always monitoring if you are stepping on a slippery rock," and I could see the ripples on the surface of the water as her fingers flowed in the space between us. "You've accepted your mother's guilt for so long, you don't know anything else. It feels scary to think about living without it."

She was making me feel like I was being whiney like a needy child, looking for sympathy, so I gave her the burden I had and I was going to give her the reality of where I was, since she knew nothing of pity.

"Now I have no one to turn to, to ask advice or to ask for support, what it's like to be a woman in this stage of life, faced with something like this. When I think about wishing she was still alive to do that, I feel bad, because she wasn't able to do that for me when she was alive. It makes me mad, that she had something she could have given me but refused to. It has taken me this long to think about what it means to be a woman, and now with ovarian cancer, I really don't know what it means to be a woman."

"I didn't know what it meant to be a woman until the birth of my granddaughter. When it is your own child, it's all about measuring up. With a grandchild, you can step back and enjoy, truly enjoy the life that unfolds, and that is where I discovered what it meant to be a woman for me."

"I think I know what you mean."

"It doesn't matter so much if you understand me. It is more important that you understand yourself. You have spent so much time trying to be what others have defined you as, you're not really sure who you want to be for your children."

The tears that slid out of my eyes were like the first drops of a storm after a long, miserable drought. Instead of soaking in, they kicked up dust and ran to lower depths, eroding with it, making an opaque slurry of the pain. It hurt to remember what I had been through. There was sadness for what I used to be and how I felt in the world when Poppa was alive. I didn't want to necessarily destroy what I was. I didn't necessarily want to be what I once was at any point of my life. Considering these things that defined me, I gave thought to how the loss of a part of one's body, not matter how insignificant, is still a loss. I surely did not know what I wanted to be, to rebuild myself as. It was all too scary.

"Those tears are like broken pieces of mirror, they reflect the part of you that is a woman and little girl and everything in between," the medicine woman said as she handed me a box of tissues. "And the part of you that is Indian."

"It is hard for me to find this pride of who I am when I distinctly recall my mother calling Indian's savages before she even knew she was one. She would say they were just like any other primitive culture who had never raised themselves to the level of written language."

"The Indian's didn't need to write down the stories, the formulas, the recipes, because they knew things changed, that we learned as time went on. Mother Earth and Father Sky would teach us new things, the lessons always there, we just hadn't been quiet enough in our spirits, we had our eyes shut at all the wrong times so we didn't see what Mother Earth and Father Sky had to teach us. And we would have to incorporate it, we would have to re-carve our history, our literature, our directions into stones or remake our literature from new birch bark scrolls. What happened if they were destroyed? If we kept it in our minds and in our words and taught each other over and over, our history would never be lost. But we didn't know a written language could be so destructive, used for such lies and destroy our people because their written language was so jealous, so greedy."

I almost flinched when she reached out to grab both of my arms into her hands. And when her flesh made contact with mine, the fear I felt was derived from the familiarity I had only felt with Poppa.

"It's okay to want things that you are entitled to," she continued. "You have a choice to not be ashamed of being Indian as much as not being ashamed of having cancer. Just like the people of the Indian Nations, we have to embrace our culture before the last remnants become nothing to wrap around us, this is the only thing that will keep us from dying. The time has come for you too."

"I don't know if I know how to do that. What I know about being Indian is only a little bit. I've forgotten what my grandfather taught me, I didn't ask him enough questions. I didn't realize how important it would be to me. Being Indian was only a secret I shared with my grandfather. I had to hide it."

"You are really no different from the rest of us then. Part of who we are, our culture, our religion is doing vision quests. The white man wouldn't even let us do it and they made it illegal until we demanded it, and made them change their law in nineteen seventy-eight. Seventy-eight, I see you recognize that wasn't very long ago. How old were you?"

"I was still a teenager. My fist child was born in eighty."

"I remember as a child, before it was made legal and going to Ghost Point, up north, for my own vision quest. We were told to listen for the drums in case the police came. We were to hide until they sounded the drums again to tell us we were safe to return."

She let go of me and fell back into her chair as if she were weary. Holding her head up, she made it clear she was still engaged with this discussion.

"You have come to me for my medicine. Do you know what this means?"

"I think it means something about how you use herbs and medicines to heal people? I don't know for sure. I only know what western medicine means, doctor's are the only ones who can diagnose."

"In the Native world it means power. My power. You have medicine, you have power. You need to find it, grow it, use it to make yourself stronger no matter how you choose to fight your cancer. It's unfortunate that so many of the white man's cultures discourage knowledge about one's own body, they want to leave it a complete stranger."

Her hands became animated again, making her words and her sentences become pictures in front of me. "I can't necessarily cure you of the cancer. But you can heal the hurt you feel. Cancer is a funny thing. It is sometimes stronger than any treatment and therapy, it defies operations and drugs and poisons that the doctors use to treat it. But sometimes the strongest, scariest of cancers disappear because of something as simple as prayers. The herbs people like me use, have a success rate that modern medicine disregards, but they will readily credit miracles, even though we know, have known for years what herbs heal sickness and destroy the bad. There is finally some respect for what we know. White man is finally realizing he doesn't have to invent everything, that if he looks close enough, Mother Earth has already provided. They have to give it the fruffy name of ethnobotany so they feel it's a worthwhile science, something they can pursue with respect."

I could only nod my head in response to all she said. I sat, listening raptly, wanting to absorb everything she said, like when Poppa would talk to me. I wanted to know the things that were not said.

"I will make a poultice for you," the medicine woman leaned toward me and said quietly. "Cancer is a strong spirit, even for our medicine. I will make it for you, I will gather special plants and pray over them. I will thank the creator for making them and ask that they heal you. I will do this, but you must work on healing your own mind, your own hurts so they don't make you weak."

"I don't know where to start." I said, feeling overwhelmed at what she was saying. I didn't know how I could possibly go back and learn what I could from Poppa that I neglected when I was a child. Then I realized, how could I learn, take back, take on a lost, lost to me, culture when I had lived in the white man's culture what seemed forever. All my life. How did I get over being ashamed of who I am and wanting to hide it? "This is scary."

"I'm glad you're scared. It means that you take this seriously, that it isn't wearing a pair of beaded moccasins and putting a couple of feathers in your hair and calling yourself an Indian. It doesn't matter what you do to the outside, being Indian happens from the inside. Find what it means to be an Indian for you."

"How do I do that?"

"I will teach you, if you want."

As difficult as it felt speaking to this woman, the brusqueness I got from her, I later concluded was her impatience with people who waste time deploring life rather than doing something about it. She had all the patience in the world to answer my questions and teach me what it meant to be Indian. I felt sad that Poppa wasn't able to share this with me and I knew it hurt him to hide what he felt. I kept whispering to myself, *seven generations, Poppa, I am remembering*. Of all I was going through, finding out and learning where I came from, my heritage, I was sure at that point, would be the most healing.

Indian Summer

I was named Patrick, Sky Lives In His Eyes, when it would have been appropriate to change it to a vast lake of water for all the tears my eyes wanted to cry. I would have never been able to dream up a scenario where I would have willingly sent the boys to a mission school. But for them to live in the shadow of their mother's deeds would only lead them on dangerous paths in a world that was now inescapable of the whites reach. I was hoping to keep them away from the bad medicine that followed their mother and the slaughter of her family and the murder of her husband.

But the ancestors spirits were strong in Big Brother. He had used their strength and guidance to take Little Brother and run away from the school. And like spawning fish, it did not matter where he had been taken; he knew where his home was. For whatever reason his parents could not reach them, he felt it was up to him to bring Little Brother home, especially since they had no way of knowing the slow death of their youngest son. They had no way of knowing the pale faces were teaching the Indian children things that were important to be a white, and encouraging the children to forget what they had been taught as important as an

Indian. It was a matter of honor that he bring Little Brother home to their mother and father, he had told me, before there was nothing left of his spirit for them to recognize.

Big Brother had come to me in the warmth of autumn, when the frost covers the earth at night, but the sun makes one more attempt before succumbing to the winds that make winter come. It was before the moon where the leaves of the trees turn colors and take flight before they reach the ground and the white children have been sent to school to sit inside all day.

He asked my forgiveness for whatever he and Little Brother had done that made me mad to send them away as punishment. Sadness overflowed my eyes that he would have thought I was punishing them rather than saving them. Then Big Brother held out a lock of Little Brother's hair.

"I am sorry again, Grandfather," he told me. "This is all that is left of Little Brother. His spirit left him before we could reach home. I think it was so scared and miserable at the school that it wanted to die too."

But everything Big Brother had done to bring Little Brother back to their parents was in vain. It was worse than seeing an animal struck with an arrow, because the animal will still fight for its life until the end. Big Brother melted before my eyes, into a despair that I could feel myself wanting to follow, when I told him both of his parents were dead. When he asked how and why, I grabbed his face in my hands and gazed into his eyes. "I speak the wrong words. They are very much alive in you." I hoped that he would see his mother and father in the reflection of my own watery eyes.

To stay alive out in the wild without his mother or father or even the dry tasting bread or watery soup with a few bits of vegetables which was the staple of the school, he survived like the animals. The morning dew would have to hydrate them for the rest of the day and into the night. He remembered his mother's instructions for eating roots, leaves and flower petals, but so much was different in the prairie, he could only dream of a clear running stream and the fish it might hold. Without his mother to guide him, they were dependant on what Mother Earth could provide them and Father Sky gave them direction during the day to follow the path of the sun.

Dizzy from hunger and tiredness, Big Brother heard the sound of the drums instead of his own heartbeat. So powerful, he could hear the chants of the men and smell the smoke from the fires. The vibrating rumbles from the clouds would bring rain, sweeping across the land and leaving the sky blue. He kept himself awake with the sounds of the drums as he protectively watched Little Brother sleep. His own body was exhausted but he had to be watchful of being found. His own body was full of energy that kept him awake. He tried scrapping the scissors clean of the rust with the sharp end of a rock.

The scissors had lain in the soft earth that had been upturned to bury another child who died at the school. The crude wooden crosses used to mark each grave were silver from the weather. New crosses were not used for new burials and Big Brother figured there were too many children dying to keep up.

He had taken a risk and disappeared from the group one afternoon when they were outside, near the cemetery. The newly turned soil was unlikely to be disturbed and the scissors would be safe until he needed them. Sister Angeline questioned him when he came back, to which he hung his head and stated he had needed to use the outhouse, but it was too far away.

With not enough to eat and finally rain that kept them wet, Little Brother became weaker and weaker. When the breath would no longer raise Little Brother's chest, Big Brother carried him until he could find a burying tree with a branch that bent at the elbow. He gently took Little Brother's plaid shirt from the school off from him, tore it into strips, and lashed the stiffening body to the branch that would be the last to hold him in its arms. He had cut a jagged lock of Little Brother's hair, enough for his parents to identify and carefully placed it in a medicine bag he created from scraps of cloth and string the Sisters had thrown away.

He had escaped the school only to be confined to the Indian Reservation. There were no fences to keep people in, but we were told to stay within boundaries the white men drew on papers, which any Indian knew the land was continuous. The assigned tribes were to stay on the land, yet they hadn't been told they were prisoners, so it was confusing when tribes went to visit others, and it fed the American's anxieties, thinking that the only reason the Indians might congregate was because they wanted to attack the whites. To heck with the whites crowding out and displacing the Indians to land deemed inferior, only to have their minds changed again, the 'pull the rug out from underneath their feet,' when really it was a round up, a concentration that made us the bulls eye to destroy not only our way of life, but end our lives too.

Even among their own tribes of Irish, German, French and English, they did not respect each other. They did not respect the earth, throwing their trash down for everyone to see like they were proud of it. It seemed like we would never get them to see us as something of value, that our slaughtered babies had been no different from theirs. I no longer had hope for them to ever change, unlike my ancestors who tried to share. And when my ancestors were unwilling to give the pale faces everything while our own starved and froze to death on the promised miracles of their Christianity, they took our values and our rituals and scrubbed them out like filth. And our retaliation made us 'savages' and 'uncivilized' while their revenge made them feel superior and justified in the eyes of their god who loved them and tolerated us.

Along with the trees the white man brought with him, trees with fruit that tasted different on every tree, my bitterness grew as I chewed the little tear drop seeds, and they released their poison, making me crazy with madness. The thoughts I had, I was told, were not Christian, that I wished a calamity, catastrophe to befall the pale faces like the pestilence they released on us. Arrogance, they had so much and justified taking what wasn't theirs. What they truly could not have they destroyed so not one could have it either. It is hard to understand their religion. It is so confusing with all of its contradictions. Just when we think we understand and we relate to our way of life, they scold us and say no, their way is the truth, ours is heathen. Peace, love, trust, are words they use to describe their Jesus, yet they don't do it themselves, maybe because they aren't capable of being as good as he was in the stories they use to teach their new generations and guide their decisions.

I told Big Brother that to survive in this world now, he would have to find a way to fit into the white world. I told him never to forget who he was, but his heritage was his to share with other natives. It was like Big Brother describing how the Sisters insisted on the boys using harsh cakes of soap that burned and left their skin dry. It was like when they were taught to raise hoes and bring them down on Mother Earth's skin, scraping it, the wind blowing over the exposed earth, drying it out. Everything we did to live by their standards would hurt us, but our only other choice was to die.

Mutual Agreements

An upstanding woman would never consider being single and earning a living in the newly tamed wilds of Michigan. But when you were a no one, a person with no family, no roots, no money, reputation was irrelevant, minute, least of all problems. An ordinary woman facing this would have smartly accepted any man who had the capabilities of supporting her financially. But Catherine was afraid of who she might become if she married just any man. She saw men as liars and full of empty promises, like her brother-in-law. To survive a world ruled and run by such meant that it was imperative for a woman to kept her mouth shut on her thoughts, better yet, not have any thoughts, for they just got a woman in trouble.

With both parents taking ill and dying, Catherine and her older sister, Elizabeth, had to fend for themselves. Elizabeth believed in what men had to offer and was dutiful in being a woman who acquiesced to male domination and ownership. The only demands she made of her future husband was to promise he would also take care of Catherine until she was old enough to be married. Elizabeth tried to be kind, but was realistic about Catherine finding a way to earn her own keep.

Becoming a teacher would allow her to feed herself until a man agreed to do that in exchange for matrimony.

As time grew shorter for when Catherine would take her exams for a teaching certificate, her sister's belly grew bigger. She watched as Elizabeth seemed to swell more with pride, more than what a baby would have distended the shape of her body to. The loss of their parents was still a huge void in their life so the promise of a new generation even excited Catherine. They made plans where Catherine would be able to help her sister recover from the baby's birth before she embarked on her trip to a teaching station where she would conduct lessons from the elementary ABC's to arithmetic, all under one roof.

But all did not work out as planned. Elizabeth became too weak to continue existing after a treacherous delivery of a baby with the feeblest cries. Catherine had no experience with birthing babies and therefore no midwife skills. Regardless, Elizabeth's husband felt he could not afford the cost of a doctor unless absolutely necessary. It was not even twenty-four hours later did Catherine lay the cold bundle next to her sister's battered body.

The anticipated drinks of celebration served a different purpose for Elizabeth's husband and he commenced to saturating his sorrows until they transformed into anger and bitterness of what he could not understand. He became drunken mad and requested Catherine's pity, then accusing her for the murder of his family and then finally to demanding that she immediately take his wife's place. With her sister's body resting eternally with the baby set in the crook of her arm in the bedroom, Catherine repelled her sister's husband by waving a butcher's knife. He could not have been sure of how many blades were really being wielded against him with his inebriated sight. He counter attacked her with profanity and insults to her lack of worth to any man.

She ran to the Reverend's house, begging for refuge. She was given inquiry to whether she realized it was improper for a young woman to be running across town with a sharp knife used for butchering hogs and daring to use it as a weapon. Furthermore, he questioned if she had considered it improper to turn away from her brother-in-law in his time of need. Catherine forced her lips to agree with a father she would not accept as hers and added that if she turned on this man once, she was useless to him forever. It would be her own burden to which she would have to make her own way in the world. He begrudgingly agreed to let her stay until she could take the next train out of town.

She told herself she wasn't running away, but just giving distance between a man who really would not expend the energy to come after a violent and homely woman as she. Honor wouldn't be worth the four hundred miles to come after her when there had to be scores of young women who would be willing to sooth his wounds from the death of his wife and child.

Catherine thought she had been toughened up, or so she thought she had been, knowing there would be some getting used to life out beyond the establishment of civilization, but not so soft and tender and delicate that she might wilt, unable to fend for herself.

But earning a living could ruin a woman too. Independence could make them think men were a novelty. Think that long enough and the woman would become a spinster. Shockingly to others who had their convictions regarding a woman's place in society, Catherine wore independence like a comfortable glove, molded to her own likeness. For some people, they reach a stage in their life that is so natural, they cannot be thought of in any other stage. School marm, spinster, roles which she seemed to be proud of. Men quit looking at her, the plainness of her features and her dress seemed to blossom into a coarseness that no one dared to disrespect, at least to her face. Catherine, what a noble name for a woman who could not be considered such after spending more than one year of her life as a schoolmarm and renting a lean to that adjoined the side of the Brook's house. There was enough privacy to not hear the noises of man and wife Brook, but close enough for them to keep a watchful eye over Catherine.

Trust was something you did not really give to females anyways. Being dependable was all together different as one had to earn the designation. She was dependable to teach school by keeping the children behaving and teaching them what they needed to know. Dependable to help those who were in need or sick. She didn't have anyone else who was dependant on her, so others felt it was a smaller sacrifice for her to give the charity of time and favor. That is how she could contribute, be an asset to the community. So when she ran off with that man, there were only a lot of whispers in her absence. It just reconfirmed that an unmarried woman could not be trusted.

In the quiet of the night, she thought she heard a baby crying. She figured the noise was her imagination or it had to be one of the animals in the Brook's barn. She dismissed it until the knock at the door startled her.

Holding the door wide open, she wasn't sure which was more pathetic, the look of defeat on the man's face or that he had chosen her to help him. Help was the only thing he was looking for with his slopping shoulders heavy with vulnerability and his head cast down in sorrow. She could only imagine why he would be at her door with a whimpering child in his arms. The wind whined at the eaves and around any loose boards on the barn, making the silence between them mournful. He obviously did not know what to say and she didn't press him. Instead, she scolded him for standing on the porch and instructed him to get that child in the house before she caught a chill of death. The glow of the oil lamp filled the room up again when she closed the door on the evening darkness from whence her visitors came from. She motioned for them to sit at the table while she arranged bread and butter.

The child was obviously hungry as her cries dulled when Catherine set the food on the table. The child looked at her father and he nodded that it was okay. She took a piece of bread and started eating it purposefully.

"You too," Catherine motioned at the man as she filled a tea kettle and set it on the stove and busied herself with stoking the coals and feeding another piece of wood to the fire. She did not stare, but kept watch of him in her periphery as he took a few slow bites and then, as if he had lost restraint, started chewing ferociously, letting it mash up enough to stick dryly in

152

his throat. Catherine figured he was hungry, but that he hadn't realized it until his mouth puckered around the dry bread.

After a silent repast of some odds and ends that Catherine had, the little girl climbed into her father's lap and curled up with her face burrowed into the folds of his shirt like an animal seeking shelter. He held her tightly against his chest.

Catherine usually held contempt for others, and in defense, kept them at a distance. Most people were greedy and if they felt they could take from you, they would. He was the first man who did not want anything from her other than help. He did not look at her suspiciously, did not look at her as if she owed him anything or should be subservient to him. She only felt his embarrassment brush against her own cheeks, making them warm. She made a point to lower her eyes. There was nothing about this man that was threatening, or giving the idea he would hurt anyone, unless it meant protecting the child in his arms.

She did not want to break him, forcing him to use humbleness to the point of groveling. Catherine knew she was capable of helping this man, but she was not sure she had the capacity to rebuild him if he went as far to tear himself apart. She knew one had to find enough prideful currency to ask for help because she knew asking someone who was weaker, who had less means, required more courage because there was also an admittance of failure.

"What brings you here?" Catherine asked him, relieving him of starting the conversation he probably dreaded.

"My wife is dead. I must take care of the child, but she needs things," he spoke, barely above a whisper. "I don't know all the things she needs."

"How did your wife die?" Catherine asked, gently. She did not know this man, but she knew of him and of his wife. The unfortunate circumstances he told her of were new.

"She was north, taking care of family when she became ill also."

"Why have you come to me?" she tried not to accuse.

"I don't know who to turn to."

"You're hiding," she knew the rumors about this couple. She knew that there was truth among the lies, but she wanted him to sort them out for her if she was going to offer any aid. In a split second of looking away from him and then back into his eyes she saw his fear for the first time as threatening. "I will help you, but first the truth. Will you?"

"I only want to protect her," he motions to the child curled up in his lap.

"If I help, will I be in danger to? If so, you must be truthful with me. Can you trust me?"

"I have no choice," his words traveled on defeat.

"You have choices. This could be the better one," she set her hand on the table between them, not for him to take, but for him to see she was earnest in helping him. "What are you hiding her from?"

"When I was young, my little brother and I were taken from our family. Taken from our mother and father. We took the train to be taken care of by father's and sisters at a mission school. They tried punishing us, beating us, whipping us, but when they could still see in our eyes what they did not like, they tried to beat our spirits," he cleared his throat like he was choking on painful memories. "My little brother was dying, on the inside. Do you believe me when I say if the inside dies, the outside will too?" He accepted the nod of her head. "I was able to escape with him. I was taking him back to our mother and father."

"That was brave," Catherine said, trying to encourage him to continue, but also trying to let him know she knew what he was risking just telling her.

"He died. I could only take a short bit of hair back to them," he shifted his arms around his daughter more securely. "I had failed."

He was not only risking his daughter's life, but was dropping his vulnerabilities across the table like the breadcrumbs that were evidence of the earlier meal.

He made the trip north with news sent that his wife had become ill with the sickness she had been trying to nurse out of her family. His wife had been returned to Mother Earth before he could make it. He returned with a two-year-old baby, so afraid of leaving her there with her aunt. He was afraid of her being sent to the Indian School. He had to get away from the reservation, far away from it and only back where his home was, could he fathom she might be safe.

"They will take her too. I cannot fail her."

"Then you have to make her invisible.

"What do you mean?"

"She has a father. She needs a mother."

"How will that make her invisible?"

"She cannot ever know who she is."

"You speak of things that just can't happen like magic, there's only me."

"You came to me for help. I will help you. I can be her mother."

"But how would I still be her father?"

"We can do it."

He looked at her with surprise understanding. "I don't come to take your life. Are you offering it?"

"Do you love your daughter?"

"Yes"

"Do you love your wife? The one who is dead?"

She watched him wince before answering, "Yes."

"If I am her mother and your wife, can you respect me?"

Tears filled his eyes, he understood the sacrifice she was offering, it was an unselfish gift. "I could never repay you."

"I only ask you to respect me."

"This won't work. Everyone knows who we are here. We can pretend, but they will never believe."

"We will have to start somewhere else. School ends in three weeks. Can you get everything you need together and see if we can't find a new home far away from here?"

"I don't know if I have enough money to do it that soon."

"I have some saved. Don't worry about the money. Just find us a new home."

Catherine touched cuff of his sleeve. "We can do this, but she can never know. No one can."

It was decided that becoming married would make their living arrangements easier and to make it less embarrassing, they created feelings of a business arrangement between them. Despite the unromantic agreement, Catherine felt giddy riding to the church with the little girl squirming on her lap. A child so small, she was not used to. With the schoolchildren, she knew her success depended heavily on being able to convince the children she was unquestionably in charge. This meant she kept her distance, she could not show the children affection, physical or otherwise, but could only show fairness. This, the children begrudgingly accepted and respected her with threats from their family to behave.

But this child, she would need to teach different things. If Catherine was to become her mother and have her forget that other woman, she would have to act like a mother and teach the child to love her. She was not sure how she would ever determine success, if there were no definitive right or wrong answers as with an arithmetic assignment. She would do this because it would be easier for him to protect the child. Being married would make it easier for her to have a life that so many men, her brother-in-law, the clergy she begged for protection, had told her that she would never have. But this marriage would be different as she would be the one providing for her husband, making him the honest one.

She indulged in thinking about what the evening might bring as she stole sideways glances at him. They never had discussed if the agreement included romantic intimacies. She knew in many cultures, arranged marriages did not allow for any pre-relationship romance or affections to develop. They were agreements of property trade, the woman being property transferred from her father's home to her new husband's house. No one talked about the sex itself, except in terms of virginity and consummation. Europe's royal families seemed to be obsessed with it, deflected though their excessive talk of lineage and heirs.

Catherine could not imagine how he might treat her. He had never touched her, except to take her hand to help her up into the wagon. As for the marriage agreement, they had not even shaken hands in acceptance. If he was gentle, it was quite possible she would let him treat her like his wife that night.

She was still a female, she justified, hungry for the touch of another's skin against hers, even if upstanding women would not allow themselves to have urges. She was too old to care what others thought of her, at least with things that did not matter. She had seen enough men and women who created a marriage to fool the rest of the world.

Mourning In The Country

Driving the roads I knew, I acted as if there was a destination but really I was just letting my mind wander over the familiar terrain. The chicory grew defiantly along the dry road sides and it smelled like summer after the sun beats down and dries out the various wildflowers and grasses that grow without the benefit of being sown by man. The gravel road crunched reassuringly under the tires of the car while periodic stones kicked up and clinked against the metal frame. The dusty breeze barely kept ahead of keeping me cool as I let my left arm extend lazily out the rolled down window of the car. I slowed down as my grandparent's house came into view and then pulled over into the ditch as I passed the barn.

The property had gone to Uncle Wes, after Grandmother died. Momma did not want to live at the farm, so Uncle Wes bought her out because he wanted to fix the place up before selling it. She bought a cute little house in town with her half of the inheritance. Uncle Wes had no interest in the farm, other than cashing it out. It was still for sale, but no one seemed interested as it sat unused, neglected for decades. A few more broken windows were apparent since the last time

I had passed by the farm. The drive was full of weeds as was the rest of the yard. It didn't seem right to park near the house like I was welcome. Heaven only knew if Uncle Wes would consider me trespassing after the stink he and my mother had after Grandmother died.

Stepping carefully, I tried not to disturb the white frilly heads of the Queen Anne's lace swaying gracefully above the purple clover popular with the bees. Looking up at the barn, I shielded my eyes from the sun with my hand, feeling like I was saluting an old general who was once respected and powerful. The red paint was weathered into the silver grain of the wood like a fading sunburn. The wild grape vine sprawled across the side like a gangly teenager, twisting its fingers around opportunities to explore new territory without the policing of scythes and hedge clippers.

Inside, the barn was cool. It could have been my imagination, but I felt its unspoken promise that it would protect me within the solid, rough-hewn timbers that held the structure up. Straw covered the floor, whispering wherever my feet moved. No one had seen reason to clean it out or sweep it up. The dust stirred and flew up to the light like insects at night. The rays of light coming from cracks between the wallboards moved and shimmered, cascading down like a spirit. Sounds were drawn upwards into echoes, like in the stone churches where the whispers gain momentum as if God is impatient and amplifies them so he can hear.

A sweet smell had permeated deep into the wood of the barn from years of housing animals and stayed as a reminder. It made me think of sorting laundry and having the scent of the person rise from their clothes, a smell that is distinctly theirs, cutting though the artificial smells of soap or cologne or perfume. Sometimes the smell of smoking or drinking will hang heavy and disguise their smell, making it into something putrid.

I climbed up the ladder to the haymow and sat against the wall that faced the house. Looking out a knothole that had long ago lost its plug, I felt like a child spying from a hidden spot, hoping to get a glimpse of something I was not supposed to see. The view from the peek hole was one I knew well, but then, it felt somehow unfamiliar. Only when I closed my eyes tight on tears could I clearly see the house freshly painted white, the neat rows of vegetables growing in the garden and my childhood of version of me playing on the patch of grass out under the oak tree.

Grandmother and Poppa were gone. Long gone, both buried so long ago. So was Momma, when she had still loved me. And Nick. Dear Nicky, the saddest death of all. For every hundred memories I had of the farm and growing up, Nick was part of ninety-nine of them. It was not so much sibling rivalry that gave the relationship distance, but the idea, the concept that we would always be brother and sister and nothing would break that bond, except for death.

I tried to conjure up that old feeling of safeness, of when I knew the boundaries of my world, where I could only go as deep as a shovel and muscle would let me. There was no reason to go further, the sky was as high as it needed to be and the county lines meant home. How I longed for that safe feeling. But would that mean giving up the pride I felt whenever I think of my grandchildren. I would have to give back the insight I gained raising my children by myself. It has not been easy, but somehow all those years I had managed to support myself and my children by selling furniture and the part-time factory cleaning.

I listened to the familiar, nostalgic, buzzing sound of cicadas waxing and waning as if a measuring gage of the hot August breezes. I could almost forget about the cancer diagnosis and how my body is rotting on the inside. I'm not arrogant enough to think I need to be preserved and live forever, but if I can't afford it, I don't even get a fighting chance?

I have to remind myself that health care is a service I have to buy, just like a car or clothes or food. Capitalism had taught me that no one deserves anything unless they work for it, too bad if one is mentally or physically less capable. I'll never be able to afford a Ferrari, but all I really need is four wheels that are mostly dependable. I can't afford to save myself into remission with this cancer, the odds aren't there, but I would like to think I could have had a chance to catch it earlier. It's a sad irony when I'm told by the know-it-all politicians on TV and in the newspapers who say it's my own fault for not going to the doctor sooner. They tell me I did not make it a priority, everyone has to make sacrifices for the important things in life. Shame on me for not sacrificing food, gas for the car, paying the bills on time, making sure my kids had clothes on their backs so I could afford to go to the doctor. Shame on me, for not landing a job that would give us health insurance. Shame on me, for not standing up to Jimmy and my mother and going to college to get a job where my job benefits could be earned by walking in high heels on the backs of the people who work with their hands and do the dirty work to make modern life easy and convenient. It isn't pity I want. I just don't want the decisions that were right to be thrown up in my face as not right or not enough.

As I walked back to the car, I fought the urge to go look in the windows of the house, looking for glimpses of Grandmother. Poppa. Nick. I remembered the song Momma use to sing sometimes when we were little, "I'm tired and I want to go home," back when I believed the only thing ailing was the swail out in the field, not knowing the secrets that hurt to keep and those same secrets that would hurt Momma.

Sitting up in the barn, I guess I finally figured out what Momma meant about feeling disconnected with her own family when Nick did not come home. Just his dog-tags and a flag Momma kept in an old trunk with brittle leather lashings at the foot of her bed, and his name eventually scribed in granite in Washington D.C. The clink of the tags I wore around my neck for a while, but they did not feel like my memories of my brother. He was the pinch in my arm, the sound of playing cards slapping together when we played rummy. He was in the patch of fine bladed grass and the dusty cornfields and the smell of the barn.

Again, Poppa's whispers of "seven generations," filled my heart with sadness, knowing Nick had died, and it meant so much more than his physical death. Now it was cancer stealing my life and making my childhood memories so far away, so long ago, cheapening it like the paper dolls thrown away when they become dirty and ripped.

Gift Of Love

It was not until Weston was born and the little girl came to see her new baby brother, did Catherine feel legitimate as the mother of both of these children she held in her arms. She had worked hard and succeeded in having the little girl believe Catherine was her mother. There was no doubt, if Catherine interpreted correctly, the little girl now believed she had been cradled in the same belly and suckled at the same breasts as baby Wes had.

It had taken several months after the marriage vows for Catherine to grow fond of Thomas and truly considering him her husband, before she dared break the barrier he had created. He hadn't even tried to kiss her much less share a bed with her. It had not been an agreement to forgo, but it had never been discussed. She never expected him to honor her sacrifice with such respect, but she wanted him to see that she was willing to give more. More than anything she wanted what husband and wife meant, not just to fool the neighbors and give his little girl a mother.

After tucking the little girl into bed one evening, she sat at the kitchen table next to him. If he noticed her across the expanse of worn wood, he did not look up from reading the newspaper.

"I've come to love that little girl," she spoke just above a whisper, wanting to interrupt his reading. He looked up and looked into her eyes, as if to see if he had heard correctly. He smiled wide and Catherine could not help herself from joining him with her own smile. She reached out and put her hand on top of his. "You too," she barely let go of the words.

His eyes welled up and when he bowed his head, tears dripped into his lap.

"I'm sorry," Catherine said and pulled her hand back.

"No," he grabbed it back, holding it between both of his hands. "When you agreed to take care of my little girl, I was astonished. I was overjoyed. I didn't feel right asking you for more."

"You don't have to ask. I want to give you. No, I want to share with you. I'm your wife now."

A year after that conversation at the table, Weston was born.

Holding the baby in her arms, she felt youthful. It seemed incongruous that she would become an old woman and have that as what her children would remember her as such. But in this very moment she had a family of her own and it fulfilled her. She had purpose, roles of wife and mother that were respected from him and the children. Not pity or scorn like when she had been called a schoolmarm or spinster. He was a different kind of man. He did not have to boss her around. He did not seem to have to feel he owned her like so many other marriages she had seen, especially her sister's marriage she had seen up close. She would not have been able to be owned anyways. In the age of suffrage, she was a woman who did not know her place within the hierarchy of males and females, was how others might describe her. But with the freedom he gave her, she was content to roam within the boundaries of wife and mother.

She didn't keep his secret as power over him, but demanded it stay a secret so they would be safe. His secret divulged would be bad for him, but Catherine was fiercely protective of the children, that nothing bad would come to them. They were innocent and what they did not know, they could not accidently divulge. It was irrefutable that she had a connection with the new baby, but she demanded it would be the same with the little girl too.

If she were to sacrifice herself to be a mother to his daughter, he would have to sacrifice by never telling the children. She had used the marriage certificate the following morning of the marriage to start the fire. "No one needs to know when we were married. The important thing is, we are." Night after night they would whisper to each other the story of who they were, as if it were a nightly prayer that would save them from being found out. He was now from up north, where his Irish family had been buried while he was a young child. He met her as a school teacher in the southern part of the state where they married and started their family. Sometimes as he repeated the story, Catherine would reach out to hold his face in her hands and she could recognize his features by touch, but there was an unfamiliar feeling and she wondered how long that would last.

Watching the tender and careful way Thomas held the new baby made Catherine cry. Most of the tears were selfish joy for herself while still a few were for the woman who had watched Thomas hold their baby girl only a few years before. She knew this was the only man she could ever love and he was the only one she wanted her children to know as father. He shifted the baby to one arm so he could wipe the tears off of her cheek.

"You have given me the greatest gift of love," he told her, filling her heart even more with contentment and satisfaction.

"I have a family now, Thomas. I have you. I have a son. I have a daughter," she said, wondering if she might have spent her life not knowing what that felt like.

"I'm so glad this makes you happy," he told her. "I just wish I could give you more, so you didn't have to work so hard. I wish I could give you more, because you deserve it."

And Catherine would recall this memory whenever she was exhausted from working the long hours on the farm, or sit at the kitchen table with paper bills demanding money they did not have. She would clench her teeth hard on this memory and urged herself on, knowing Thomas was standing next to her, working just as hard to make their life as a family. And she hardly needed the daily reminder that her gift of love was her family they had created together.

Seven Generations

I decided to embrace my Indian heritage after seeing the holistic doctor. It had been a secret I had shared with Poppa, but I didn't realize what it meant. It wasn't just blood we shared, but also a heritage he had to give up and a way of life I would never know. But I couldn't lay blame on myself entirely when I had packed up all my memories of Poppa for safekeeping when Momma completely melted down, when she damned me, her own daughter, for what she saw as a treasonous act against her. Poppa had committed me to keeping the secret, and when the kids at school clowned around and made fun of Indians, I let a smile cover my face, denying the part of me numbed by humiliation. Maybe I hadn't been any better than Momma who had shunned being an Indian and looking down on them all those years before she knew.

Talking with this doctor gave me the courage to embrace my heritage that had become so shameful. I decided if I didn't let myself be true to myself now, I never would be. I was surprised that it could feel more comfortable to admit than trying to hide it for a change. By identifying as being Native American, I was part of something larger than the family that I once had. Would people see me differently? Could I embrace something that I avoided for decades? Could I quit pretending that I wasn't something else? Finding answers to my questions meant I had to discover who I truly was on the inside, but I also had to consider who I was not allowed to be on the outside all of these years.

It took a lot of thought to decide if I was not going to pursue cancer treatment because of the money it would take to treat. I don't have the money and I did not want to leave a legacy of unpaid bills for my family to be responsible for. Another Native teased me that my true heritage was surfacing, saying any Native was leery of taking anything from any government agency, even if it was state government sponsored health care. In addition, treatment doesn't necessarily mean a good quality of life, but of the limited days I have, I would rather let my body decline as it may, rather than subjecting it to sickening treatments. On the other hand, I didn't want to be like the people who were scared to death of dying and spent the rest of their lives chasing cures, promises of medicines and eternal youth.

While working to find a peace of mind with my decisions to forego treatment and to be at peace with my eventual death, what really bothered me was the fact that I didn't have anything to pass down to my children and grandchildren. I had nothing I could give to my children or grandchildren that felt all that important or which they might think was important. I didn't want what was once my life to become a hole, where all that's left would be a vacancy full of sadness and over time become filled up with other distractions and forgotten. Sometimes the space a person takes up is already allocated, so when they do pass, there is no loss, which is unfortunate to think that a living person's life can be so expendable. By embracing my native roots, I felt that I finally had something that I could give them.

One thing that surprised me while searching for my native roots and learning about native ways, is it allowed me to soften, let me feel emotions, some good, some bad. I had been so worried I wouldn't be accepted by other Natives. What would other Indians think of me, the bona fide, looks-like, acts-like, raised-like? Would I have to submit to more taunting, rather than being able to laugh along with a joke so I could fit in? Try to make others forget who I was, but it was me who was the only one fooled? Some I knew, would not accept me, but I was prepared, having the experience with Momma, when she got old and sick and how she pushed me away and distrusted my motives for helping.

I read everything I could on cancer. Not so much the cures or therapies, but where and how it started in one's body. Being a child of the DDT era made me sad as I thought of the swail on my grandparent's farm. I finally realized why Poppa and Grandmother scolded us as kids for playing in the mist from the chemical sprayer pulled behind the farm tractor. I never realized how hard it must have been for Poppa to live in the white world and suppress the native world that was his. It had to be his native background that made him aware of the chemicals deemed good for the crops by the white world, was bad for the earth. Oh, how I miss him more today, more than I ever did after he died. I have done a few things to remember Poppa, but not enough.

When Poppa started getting weak, Grandmother

would have me stay with him while she did errands in town. We would spend hours sitting on the back porch while he smoked his pipe. It was different than the fast burning cigarette smoke of my mother's cigarettes. Pipe smoke was rich and smooth, its curves swelling around my head. Poppa would often just stare at me while he held his pipe clenched between his teeth.

"In seven generations, I will be fully alive," he mused quietly.

"What does that mean?" I asked.

"It means that your mother is a generation, you and your brother are a generation, your children will be a generation, your grandchildren will be another generation. Your great grandchildren and their children. If all of them are born, I will continue living."

"What if I don't have children?"

"Then in seven generations, you will have been forgotten. Your death really is in the break of your seven generations."

After that initial conversation, I could seen him mouth, 'seven generations,' whenever he looked at me or my brother or cousins.

"Tell me more," I would beg him.

"What do you want to know?"

"Everything," I said so innocently, back when I only knew shame for saying a naughty word. To know everything was important to me. With the sweetness of the pipe smoke wrapping around both of us, closing in until we were one, he would tell me more.

"The pale faces wanted everything they saw, like babies who don't understand that nothing belonged to them, when it was all on a long-term loan from Mother Earth. We were just borrowing. Those who got ownership in their heads were a little loony."

I didn't understand what he meant, but I didn't want him to quit talking. I want his attention.

"Just like young kids who want to touch the fire and even after being told not to, they still wonder why it burned them. Respect. That's something else they wanted, but they don't realize they got to give it to get it back in return. They wanted the land, the waters, the animals who lived on both. They even wanted the souls of the Indians. The only thing they were not able to reign into their control was the sky. The Indians didn't want anything from the pale-faces and ended up losing everything. I'm telling you, Anna, they took everything away and thought they had conquered us. I know it's wrong when you have to hide who you are all your life, but as long as I keep the knowledge and pass it to you, and hopefully the seed that has lain dormant for so long can still grow and flourish at the right time."

I loved hearing those covert stories Poppa would tell about the Indians. I felt like I was learning more about myself when I heard them, could see them unfurling in my mind as his fingers swayed back and forth in front of him as if he was drawing me pictures of all the words he spoke.

"I want to know all the stories, Poppa," I would tell him, cuddling up in his frail arms.

"I will tell you all the stories I can, my dear child, the ones that are mine to share with you. Not all stories are meant to be given away for entertainment or even as a lesson if the person in the story is the one who is to learn. There are a lot of stories, Anna, lots that you will never know, and those are the ones that need to be respected. But the stories I do tell you, don't forget.

Someday you need to tell them so we may live. Seven generations. Don't forget."

Learning about myself as a native, I realized I had to learn about those around me without their help. By destroying the ideal of who I thought Poppa and Grandmother were and then recreating it, I was able to understand Grandmother had such a love for Poppa. It took a much longer time for me to understand that she could have such a fear for him that she must have felt fragile against the world, knowing if they shared who he was, it would become his vulnerability, negating him as a person of worth in the eyes of their own community. It didn't matter how honest or hardworking someone was if there was a reason to look down on them.

It's like listening to an old song that you remember hearing on the radio, played at a different time in your life, when the future was full of memories yet made, and so many hurts had yet happened, and you can taste only the sweetness, not knowing there is something bitter, more pithy to exist. Only when you're older can you transport yourself into that far away, long ago moment and know the sweetness of the moment is even better because the tempering of the bitter.

Coming to terms with my own mortality, I realized that when someone dies, with each death, all others are relived, all the guilt, the promises broken, not by my own decisions, but because death made the decision. Promises to call, to meet for lunch or to visit when better are all broken. Death then takes all those chances ever to apologize and to be forgiven. It isn't until someone dies is it realized that they took a wealth of knowledge with them. It's all lost for eternity. Yet it's a chance for some of the living to grab a chance at the limelight, to be the first to announce, be the one who has charming antecedents to share. And the living keep living and hording their present immortality. And that is when I realized healing my soul was more important than healing my body.

My children were angry with my decisions to not purse medical treatment. And when I wanted to talk about my death, they said I was pressuring them. I told them I would die one way or another. In a weak moment, I accused them of being afraid of my death and being selfish not to acknowledge my death as much as my life. "I'm going to be dead a long time longer than I'm going to be alive."

"It's unhealthy to dwell on your death, Mom."

"I don't want you to be sad," I was earnest in telling them.

"How can you say that?" my daughter accused. "I know we've had our differences, but don't throw that in my face."

"Honey, you're not listening. That's not what I'm saying at all. I want us to have peace with each other. I want to know when I take my last breath that I have you and your brother and my grandchildren. I don't want you thinking or wishing there was more you wished you could have done for me. Having a family is all I will ever need."

I continue to explain to my children how I feel, as they need constant reassurance that it is okay for them to accept my decisions. For the new baby, I knew that I would be gone before she would be able to comprehend anything I could say. Somehow I wanted to let another one of my generations know the knowledge that I had gained in my lifetime. I wanted that baby that was due any day to know who I was and what I wanted her to become.

I thought of Poppa, most likely forcing Grandmother to sit at the kitchen table and write his words down. It was so important that before the memory of him dissolved from this world, that those who he loved, knew the secrets he had kept. I had no secrets that I could share that I felt would give my new grandchild clarity to her life, but I played with a pencil between my fingers and curled the edges of the pretty paper with my thoughts before I wrote what I knew I wanted to share.

Baby girl, all you know right now is innocence and for the rest of your life you will lose it. So I beg you to hold it tight in your fists you wave in the air and dream about it behind those delicate petals when your eyes are closed. It is your personal innocence when lost, makes you weak and it is your innocent view of the world when lost, makes you strong. You will not listen to the old women around you, what do they know, you will think. You will disdain us for letting wrinkles form around our eyes, but it is from years of looking into the glare of life. You will disdain us for the soft bellies we wear, but it is because we walked heavily, knowing life beyond ourselves, during the months before you were born.

No, we won't ridicule you for what you don't know. We won't tell you of everything that steals your innocence. We will only hold you tight in our minds, offering comfort and protection for the tender parts of your heart that will recall only a whisper of baby contentment as you grow older. We do this because you

*offer us hope, another chance, that those perfect little
ears will never hear hurtful words, those soft baby feet
will never journey roads cobbled with sharpness.*

*We look at your unblemished skin, knowing our
souls were once as pure and smooth, and we can't stop
caressing your chubby little legs and cheeks sweeter
than any apples. It would be so selfish for us to not
want you to become a woman. It is only when strands of
old color your hair might you understand that for all
the innocence you have lost, you have to replace it with
understanding   and   compassion   and   sheer
determination.*

*So, baby girl, you hold onto that innocence for
as long as you can. You wear it as the fragrance of
mother's milk and embrace it in the curves of your lips
when you smile, because you know what innocence is.*

It was a pilgrimage for my family to the
Sleeping Bear Dunes. I had been there as a child, but
now I had another reason to go. I wanted to teach my
grandchildren the story of the dunes. It was as much a
part of their history as what they would learn in school
textbooks.

I had visited Sleeping Bear Dunes as a child, but
the only thing I remember from that time is how Nick
came down the dune too fast, thinking his legs would
carry him safely to the grassy edge. He tumbled head
over heels, down the steep incline, reaching the bottom
with a mouthful of sand.

We had grown up in what felt like the middle of
the state, which I believed to be the center of the
universe and everything else revolved around it.
Hugged by waters that are sometimes considered just as

dangerous as oceans, I was insulated, centered. It took almost an hour to drive to the next state. Another nine hours going the other way. At the shores edge, while on vacation with Grandmother and Poppa we could see Canada across the water on a clear day. It did not seem so foreign of a country, but seemed like a bigger version and a more encompassing wilderness of the Upper Peninsula.

It had to be the birth of my second granddaughter in the spring that kept me going to make it to this summer. If her birth had happened in the fall or the early winter, I may have not made it through the winter with those cold and grey days, void of any hope. Whenever winter was coming, Poppa would speak of those that did not want to try and make it through the hardest season. It was important to me to take all of my grandchildren north, so I waited for the new baby to be not so new and let her experience what I wanted to share with them.

I returned to the Dunes, so my grandchildren could experience the grandeur of billions of grains of sand creating a mountain range on Lake Michigan's east shore. Nothing can compare to the flatness of the sand in a sandbox in the back yard and the realization that the Dunes are alive with their constant motion. Seeing the blueness of lake merge seamlessly with the blueness of the sky was a great reward after climbing high enough to pick out the baby bears, the two small islands to the northwest. But there was disappointment also, as I raised my hand to shield my eyes, I became aware of the many more valleys and hills to cross before reaching the deep, deep blue that makes me forget I am thirsty.

After a half hour of trekking, we felt Lake Michigan was no closer, yet a freighter off in the horizon had made it past one of the islands. I encouraged everyone, wanting them to experience the water doing its part in pushing the sand away from where the sun sets, even though they have played on other sandy beaches. I told them they were looking at sand that I thought was prettier than any beach in the Caribbean. Only here does the beach grass grow determined, trying to convince the sand grains to cling to its rooted embrace. Only here can the romance of the Indian folk lore take one back to the beginning of time.

Hulking metal freighters in the distance added some kind of perspective to the little island that make the boats look like bathtub toys. The wind coming off the lake whispered in my ears until I heard a roar of high-powered engines. I looked out at the horizon and saw fighter jets. They were flying low enough to make sure the people back on planet earth could see their silhouette reposed against the blue sky. The faces of hikers turned skyward and shining eyes looked up to see the silver cut through the sky.

I felt the vibrations of the jets and the vibrations of my racing heart. Blood surged through the avenues of arteries and veins, propelled by adrenaline and the wonder of the powerful noise cutting through the sound waves in the sky and the phallic shape so ingrained in our psyche as power. It was just the National Guard on its monthly weekend of maneuvers. It was my children pointing for their children to look at the war planes flying overhead practicing peace. And I wondered, how many times those silver beasts would comb the sky overhead, before they would become another sound in their life taken for granted.

The jets disappeared towards the mainland and I pointed out the islands in the distance to my grandchildren. I tell them the story of the mother bear and her twin cubs who had to run away from the forest fires in Wisconsin. Coming to the lake they had to swim, mother bear is what we stand on and her cubs are still out at sea. They were so little they couldn't make it, so their momma stayed with them forever. I don't know how much I can teach my children and grandchildren when I am still learning that stories like this are more than amusing tales, because they explain more about who we are as Native American Indians, understanding that our heritage is so, so precious for us to learn and never forget.

We finally make it, worn out, but delighted to have arrived. It is a modern day pilgrimage. After regaining some of my energy from the hike, I called the grandchildren away from the edge of the sand where the water flirts coyly, but with a sensually that has taken thousands of years to learn.

"Come, come, before the morning is over. I want to teach you the Morning Prayer." The sun is overhead so it makes it a little difficult to determine the four directions of Mother Earth. The water is to the west and where we traveled from is to the east, is how I guide myself as I draw a circle in the sand with my bare toes, initialing each direction for the children. I take the baby in my one arm and grab the next littlest hand in mine and stop at the E. My oldest granddaughter holds my elbow from behind.

"This is the prayer circle. I've made this for you today. One day you will be able to close your eyes and stand in the circle without it being there. Grandson, do you know what the E and the S and the W and the N stand for?" He tells me what they are and I have each of the other grandchildren repeat it. "We are going to enter the circle from the east." I direct them and I pull them close to me as we face the dunes. I feel a shiver go through me as the wind presses against my back, but I know it has to be more than that with the sweat beading on all of our foreheads. The grandchildren are not only quiet but there seems to be a calmness to them that is usually absent even when they are silent. "I'm going to say the prayer a sentence at a time and I want you to repeat it with me when I say it again." I instruct them.

"Thank you Mother Earth for what you have given me."

"For my existence and for another day."

"Thank you Father Sky, for what you have given me."

"For the rain and the light and the dark."

"Ancestors, spirits, beings of the East."

"Thank you for new beginnings."

"For a new day, for new opportunities."

I turn and they follow.

"Ancestors, spirits, beings of the South."

"Thank you for healing and the passion of life."

"Help us to appreciate what it is to be alive each new day."

They anticipate the turn, but wait for me.

"Ancestors, spirits, beings of the West."

"Thank you for your wisdom."

"Help us to gain the wisdom to know what it is to be alive each new day."

We turn together.

"Ancestors, spirits, beings of the North."

"Thank you for your understanding."

"Help us to gain the understanding to use the wisdom of knowing what it is to be alive each new day."

"Good job, my little ones. Should we do it again?" I asked and they are uncharacteristically compliant. We do it again, turning in our huddle to each of the four directions before I lead them out of the circle. They break into a scattered run as each of their feet step over the threshold of the east. I still feel a little self-conscious about doing it. I know they tire easily and I think that they are bored with it because they don't realize the importance yet, and I feel sad.

"I guess we can quit for now," I said as kindly as I could, trying to keep any hint of blame out of my voice. I turned to my children and speak to them. "I'm sorry for injecting native ways into everything we do now. I know you are used to doing just the normal things."

"It's important to you, Mom. It's okay," my daughter replies. This is my daughter who was bitter it seemed like her whole life, for what I could not provide. Now that I'm dying, she speaks to me as if she were wearing kid gloves. She truly is sad that my death is so near. I sit down on a blanket she had smartly thought to bring and spread out on the sand.

And I am hit with a hurtling child landing in my lap. My grandson looks up at me with playfulness in his face.

"Thank you for doing this with me," I say and plant a kiss on his sweaty forehead.

He looks up at me and says, "It's a part of us, so we have to learn about it."

I grab him tight and shake him in my embrace as my muscles contract with the heaving of my crying and tears explode out of my eyes. And I know my children and grandchildren will have to learn from others in the Native community, but at least they will have the memories of me, their first memories of ceremony will be of me.

Seven generations. Don't forget.

ABOUT THE AUTHOR

Emma Donaldson is an enthusiast for good food and the great outdoors. Within the boundaries of the state where she resides, she can find both and she believes it is hard not to be romantic and sentimental when one calls Michigan home.

Made in the USA
Charleston, SC
22 December 2014